Felicity

Felicity

A NOVEL

Maggie Barrett

2019

This is a work of fiction. Names, characters, businesses, organizations, places, events, and incidents either are the product of the author's imagination or are used fictitiously. Any resemblance to actual persons, living or dead, events, or locales is entirely coincidental.

Hardcover edition: 978-1-64713-938-4
Paperback edition: 978-1-64713-955-1
eBook edition: 978-1-64713-972-8

Printed in the United States of America

To my sisters, in order of appearance:
Brenda, Vivian, Agathe, Pip, Madeleine, Scout, and Kate

Felicity

1

FELICITY HAS HAD ENOUGH. At the moment, it's literary death that's pissing her off. She slams the book shut at page 173. Who gives a shit about a handful of old fictitious characters and their modes of inevitable demise? Cheer the fuck up! she wants to yell, not so much at the characters as at the acclaimed author whom she herself has long admired. Is that really the best you can do? Are you telling us, after an illustrious, pushing-the-envelope career, that the end is nigh and boring?

That Felicity holds a grudge against the publishing world and herself for being a failed writer is something she is aware of and it frightens her. Over the past year or so she's begun to taste bitterness blooming like mold and is appalled that her own inevitable demise might carry her off like a dry twig before she finds acceptance, let alone gratitude and inner peace.

The sun is pushing its way through the cobbled alley across from the village bar where, before heading to the supermarket, she sits with a cappuccino and the dreary book. She's about to shove it in her bag but instead, with spiteful glee, rams it into the café's already full garbage can, tempted for a moment to take a photo of it and send it to the author's publisher.

On her way home through the spring-lit hills to the old renovated barn where she lives with her husband, she feels herself blazing with anger; the light is new and green, a signal to go ahead, let it all out. As she goes into the final curve, the first sentence comes to her, unbidden and volatile. . . . Felicity has had enough.

Unlike the characters in the book she'd slammed shut, Felicity hasn't had enough of living. Sure, there are times she's had enough of the world, who hasn't these days? Who'd have thought that by age seventy, one would have to reckon with a fascist American government and Brexit at the same time as coming to terms with personal failure. And who the fuck had decided that the endgame should be unfair, arthritic, acidic, judgmental, and tiring; that the highest hurdles would be placed closer together for the final lap?

Fueled with violent green energy, Felicity itches to get to her desk and begin writing her next and hopefully final novel; the one she's always wanted to write. Felicity wants to write her way out of the corner and she doesn't give a toss if nobody reads it. Better for them if they don't because there will be no fictitious characters in this novel. She'll allow one courtesy to each; each will be christened anew, but their identities will lie unredeemed upon the page.

2

AS FELICITY ROUNDS THE LAST BEND of the dirt road, she feels the beginning of a skid; the gravel is dry and treacherous. Glancing in the rearview mirror, she sees the inevitable cloud of dust obliterating what a moment ago had been green fields stained with poppies. Does the past always have to disappear in a cloud of dust? She eases her foot off the accelerator and pulls up just before the garden gate over which an arch of Nahema roses and jasmine are pushing their perfumed blossoms into the world.

Reaching into the back seat for her grocery baskets, her black jeans brush up against the Peugeot, which deposits a smear of putty-hued dust all over them. Bloody hell. They'd just washed the car yesterday and less than twenty-four hours later the damn thing is completely covered in dust. White roads they call them. White, my arse.

A basket in each hand, she kicks the gate closed behind her, except that it doesn't close; a string of rainy days having swelled the wood. Oh, good. Another chore to add to the list: shave the gate, spray the roses, pull the weeds, replace the wheel on the barrow, bring in the firewood, hang out the laundry, unpack the groceries, make lunch. With each chore her inner fume gathers heat. And what exactly is your problem, Felicity? When did you start becoming so angry? What's with all the constant griping?

She dumps the baskets outside the door, unable to face the interior of the house, as if it might go up in flames if she took her own emotional interior there. Sitting in one of a pair of wicker chairs, she takes a deep breath and on the exhalation a few tears slide down her cheeks. Really, when did she start becoming such an angry person? She tries to see herself as a child, scans the terrain of childhood searching for that first spark of anger that would indicate the beginning of a life of increasing rage. What she finds is a lost child. Shy, yet full of imagination and possibility. A foundling taken in by the wicked witch, whose disappointment at having adopted an imperfect daughter gradually changed to rage. The child for whom laughter carried punishment. The wet knickers proof that this child was a dirty child whose nose must be rubbed into the knickers' crotch until the urine turned to perfume.

An early bee hovers over a nearby bush of Cubana roses, searching for an opening from which to retrieve pollen, but the buds' tiny green fists remain closed. Right, time to fertilize. Add that to the list. She feels her lips fold in on themselves, sees herself reflected in the thin line of her mother's mouth and feels the bitterness passed between them without the benefit of shared blood.

3

OF COURSE, she hadn't gone straight to her desk. There was never a direct line between the urge to write and the actual sitting down and doing it. Unlike her highly successful spouse and, she presumes, every other successful man, Felicity has a ritual of guilty punishments that must be put ahead of her need to create. Well, actually, she had gone straight to her desk, uncapped her pen and then remembered she'd left the groceries outside with the gelato melting in the midday sun which, of course, was hotter than it should be partly because of the atrocious mess humans were making of the planet and partly because, well, of course, there *had* to be something beyond her control that made it impossible for her to do what she wanted to do. And that, she fumed, as she put the groceries away, was why her spouse was so highly successful; because he always put himself first. She knew this wasn't completely true. Knew, actually, that he did more than many a man when it came to sharing the household duties. Still . . .

She takes the lid of the gelato. Fucking soup. Of course it is. Gelato is her last remaining addiction and this is her first container since winter, so of course it's ruined. And of course, *his* chocolate biscuits are fine. He doesn't do gelato anymore. Makes his bum fall out, he says. She ponders the coffee liquid as she pours it down the drain. Looks like his bum has fallen out without the gelato ever entering his body. Oh, Felicity, just shut up and go to work.

She climbs the stairs to what had once been the hayloft, its beamed ceiling casting a warm amber light on the old farm table that is her desk and a sudden surge of gratitude fills her. And isn't that what she wants to feel? Hasn't her life come to a place of beauty in a country they'd fallen in love with the first year they'd fallen in love with each other? And must the gratitude also be raged against? Appearing now at the very moment she'd chosen to start a new novel? A novel born of the need to write herself out of the corner? Where was the corner now, when she needed it? Was there nothing to count on?

Wow. Neat trick, Felicity, how to turn gratitude into anger. She looks over to her husband, who is engrossed in whatever the fuck is engrossing him and decides to rechristen him Spouse. Uncapping her pen once again she inks the first sentence onto the page and knows she's in for a dangerous ride.

4

FELICITY KNOWS A THING OR TWO about dangerous rides, having been nearly killed in one some twenty-seven years earlier. Two and a half weeks after she'd met Spouse, actually. Spouse having appeared at sunset, literally out of the blue, or as he would call it "the blue hour." His steed a silver racing bike; his silver curls evident beneath the helmet's rim.

Not yet two years sober and newly divorced for the fourth time, Felicity had taken a week's vacation on Cape Cod. Smug in the knowledge that her man-magnet would be null and void in a gay town, off season, she had pictured herself happily alone at the water's edge; a journal, some paints, and a few candles her only company. Ha! Know-it-all. It was only day three when Spouse appeared, proving her wrong once again.

Softened by sobriety and her own successful career as a painter and salon owner, she let herself fall slowly and with a certainty that had nothing to do with need and everything to do with inevitability. For here was an equal. Here was a man with the capacity to listen. Here was a man with quiet elegance and gentle sensuality. So what if he didn't have a sense of humor. Kindness might suffice.

They'd spent the rest of her vacation swimming, kayaking, biking, holding each other in the hollow of a dune while watching the clouds form themselves into the gods neither believed in. At the end of the week, when she drove the three hundred miles home alone, she felt the line reeling out behind her, felt him quiver at the other end and knew that they would reel each other in again and again for the rest of their lives. And so it went.

The following weekend she took the bus to New York City to be with him. The weekend after, he drove upstate to her. The crash happened on the third weekend, the day before she was to see him again in the city. She was on her way to a friend's house near Woodstock. The road splattered with rain-slicked leaves, the leaves jeweled with autumn's colors. A shiny, black four-wheel drive vehicle in front of her suddenly pulled off the road without signaling. Asshole, she'd muttered. Asshole indeed. What Felicity had thought to be a hastily executed roadside stop turns out to be the beginning of a reckless, but not wreck-less, U-turn. She sees immediately where she is headed. Sees the red pinstripe along the side of the other vehicle. Her foot hard on the brake. Arms straight. Steering wheel in a death grip. Spine pushed back against the seat in an instinctive attempt to avoid the unavoidable impact that races up her arms at fifty-five miles an hour, the red pinstripe a line between before and after, the front of her white Honda Civic folding up like a fancy napkin, the pain ENORMOUS. The world stopped. Every bird ceasing its song and in the silence she hears her tiny voice, "Help me." She tries to move but her body will not comply. Paralyzed from the neck down she hears her mother's voice coming toward her over the adjacent field. "Told you so."

Closer now. "You should have known this would happen." The voice almost at the roadside fence. "Just when your life was getting good." The mother who had driven her away as a teenager was coming for her now and if she makes it over the fence Felicity knows she'll die. She tells her mother to fuck off. A bird sings.

5

FELICITY LOOKS AT THE FIRST SENTENCE and thinks maybe she could just begin and end with that sentence and call it Flashier Fiction. She's so had it with aging writers and their joyless journey to the grave and has no intention of becoming one of them. Frankly, she resents the hell out of them. How could they have achieved literary fame for all those decades only to fizzle out in the final lap like a wizened dick dribbling spit instead of jizz and *still* get published? And how could she herself have escaped death in the prime of her life only to arrive at her own endgame filled with anger? Well, duh. The answer was because she'd spent the years between near death and nearing death writing stuff no one wanted to read. Wouldn't that piss you off? What the fuck had she been thinking? Had she actually been thinking or merely telling herself a story? What's the story, Felicity?

An itch starts between her shoulder blades. She tries to reach it with her left hand and failing, puts down her pen and tries with the right, but the itch remains out of reach thanks to four fused vertebrae. How much else has remained out of reach since she broke her neck? And how, if she'd had the courage to survive *that*, had she not been able to achieve success with her second chance at life? Questions, questions, questions. She feels like Alice in Dunderland.

"What's for lunch?" Spouse's voice, whose gentle tone belies his Bronx origins, shoots down her spine like a bolt of lightning taking the itch with it. She turns to him. Sees his sweet face, eyebrows perpetually arched in boyish amazement. Feels the tug of love, the beginning of a thought, the possibility of escape or enlightenment. There, before her, sits success. Not his, but theirs. Evidence of a successful marriage. Could that not be enough? Which way to turn; surrender or pick up arms? Could shared success be enough or must she insist on her own?

"How the hell should I know?" she snaps and turns away as the tears come.

Of course, she could laugh at it now and make others laugh when telling the story of her "accident." What she never told was the doubt. Had it been an accident? Obviously the other driver was to blame. Even the insurance company finally agreed on that. But it would be years before Felicity would have the thought that choice existed. Even in that split second. Swerve left? Or swerve right? If she had swerved right she may have run off the road but would have avoided impact with the guy in the black Blazer with a red pinstripe. But she had swerved left. Had the laws of attraction been at play? Was it the red pinstripe that had seduced her? Oh, Felicity, give yourself a break. Funny. That's exactly what she had done. C5 and C6 fractured. Instant paralysis. Royal drag. World gone quiet. Mother fucked off. Bird singing. Other driver coming to her car window. "I want my friend," she'd whispered, referring to her spouse-to-be. If he would just be her friend and kiss her once in awhile it would be all right. It'll be all right, sang the bird.

6

LUNCH. TEARS. GUILT. Shame. Anger. Resentment. What a smorgasbord! Guilt and Shame for starters. Turning away from Spouse, she jumps up from her desk.

"I'll make it," she says.

"We'll make it together," Spouse says.

Maybe tongue on wry, she thinks, biting hers in order not to voice that which is stuck in her craw. Bitterness, such an *amuse bouche*.

Actually, how about for starters we do something together besides making lunch? Remember making love? Remember the mango? So ripe it undressed itself before you undressed me. The lusciousness of its pulp, its vivid orangeness, slathered on her skin, her skin still crêpe-free, his tongue all over her and in her, mango juice blending with vagina juice. What a smoothie.

"Tuna salad?" Spouse offers, and a laugh rips out of Felicity because really isn't it all just so bloody absurd? She turns back to her desk to cap her pen and starts downstairs.

"How about you make the toast?" he says.

I *am* toast, she thinks.

The thing is, Felicity has it good and she knows it. Married to a successful artist, who, after years of her living in his world had had the kindness, the decency, the courage goddamn it, to agree to living in Europe for a year. And at the end that year Spouse had said, "Why only a year?" And she'd let him have the idea all to himself, although it was what she'd hoped for all along. The deal had been that barring family emergencies, Spouse could not return to New York during that year. Felicity's thought being that if she could keep him away from New York for a year he'd be able to detox from it.

Look, she wasn't a monster. She knew he was a born and bred New Yorker. A Bronx Boy. Seventy-five years in his city. Summers on Cape Cod. And she, of all people, knew what it was like to feel the cellular identification and pull of place.

Nineteen she'd been when she left England with a cheap blue suitcase and eleven Canadian dollars. Dreaming of a two-year, round the world trip, just like all the Aussies whom she'd met in London had done. Her running away from home to live in London. Sixteen years old. Starved for love. Fucking half of Australia before she left for Vancouver, the first leg of her global tour. How was she to know that her need for love would keep her there for four years during which time she would marry and divorce Spouse Number One and spend the last six months of her Canadian adventure in a mental institution? Desperate for love? Ya think? Why else, at twenty-three, would you hook up with a rich, forty-four year-old inmate who was taking the guided LSD treatment? And then run away with him to Manhattan? Live in a two-story loft, serve Hungarian goulash to him and his friend fifteen minutes after reading the telegram informing her that her father, who she was yet to find out was not her father, had died two weeks earlier. The goulash was incredible. The grief too much to swallow, washed down with wine, and off you go Felicity. Dream of Daddy every year, running after him in a hospital corridor, catching up with him, holding his hand. Dream over. Why not have a *ménage á trois* with acid-head and his friend and then move in with *trois*, marry him, bear him a stillborn daughter and lose custody to him of the second, so alive daughter? Game over Felicity. You are *never* moving back to England.

So yeah. Another two husbands before Spouse, sometimes known as Number Five. A total of forty-seven years living in North America longing for home. Twenty-plus years of it in Manhattan with Spouse. His city. His home. Not her city. Never her home. But she understood, and the part of her that was still intact at the core, the core that refused to let the rot of negativity eat away at it, that part, the part that would always choose love over place, that part of her hung in there until the kind heart of Spouse finally saw her sacrifice and agreed to a year in Europe.

And now here she is, living on a farm in Europe, surrounded by gobsmacking beauty, making a garden from bare rock, speaking a new language, and still writing novels nobody wants.

Nobody wants? Add "me" to that sentence and you have her lament since she was three. Who gives a shit if she's written that before? Hear it again. Like the poet Stanley Kunitz, ninety years old, standing on the stage at the 92nd Street Y, calling out to his father. Five-year-old Stanley standing on his roof calling out to his father. The father who committed suicide while Stanley was still in the womb, who couldn't hang in long enough to look at the face of his son as he entered the world. A look that might have been enough to live for. Stanley, ninety and five in the same moment. On the stage and on the roof at the same moment, calling out to his daddy, "*Look for me, Father . . . on the roof of the redbrick building. . . . I'm the boy in the white flannel gown.*" The lament burned into him at birth. Nobody wants me, burned into Felicity at birth. Felicity riding her tricycle up and down the hall of the house of her pseudo-parents crying, "Nobody wants me, nobody wants me." Hearing them laugh at her in the kitchen. Well, get this Stanley: My mum looked at me and *still* walked away.

They opt for salad and last night's leftover seared tuna, sliced on the side. Felicity already has the salad made and the table set while Spouse is still meticulously slicing the tuna. She watches him with a mixture of exasperation and bemused appreciation. Are we all like this, she wonders? All of us focused in the one narrow lane we choose or are born into? And does that make a difference, to be born a natural at something, or to choose it? Does it matter? You could say Spouse was born to it, saw it, chose it by age twenty-four, and had been perfecting his art ever since, much like he now trims the tuna of any defect.

Defect? Had her blood mother seen a defect in her? Searched for one even, in order to be able to walk away? For sure her adoptive mother had seen defects galore and mercilessly pointed them out for the first sixteen years of Felicity's life. Can an infant be scarred by the superimposition of false defects? And why was it easier to blame the adoptive mother than the blood one? Or, as Felicity had written—in the play she'd performed, the one everyone loved but nobody wanted—in which she referred to her mothers as *"the one a saint and the other a martyr."* And is this what I'm doing to my spouse, she wonders? Finding fault where none lies in order to keep my distance? Well, in all fairness, the man was excruciatingly slow when it came to anything other than his art. But hey, seems he has the winning strategy: He has you, Felicity, and success and before that a childhood with doting parents. So why bother competing? That race is over and won. And besides, *he* wants you for god's sake. Does it really matter if he doesn't always want you the way you want him to want you? He's still here, isn't he? When your mother tried to make it over the fence and finish you off, this man brought you a peach. Came to the hospital carrying a peach that would ripen to perfection by the time they took you off the morphine and the antibiotic drip. Peach juice dripping down her chin. The halo vest already screwed into her head. C4 through C7 fused with the rib of a dead man. Adam's rib she calls it. Maybe she should have changed her name to Eve.

She'd grown up as Phyllis. Could hear her "mother" calling out to her on the street in her fake-cheery, fake middle-class voice, "Phiii-lisss." What kind of name was that? She'd hated it growing up, and when at age twenty-five she found out she was adopted, was not who she'd come to believe she was, then, it almost made sense that the mother who'd never *felt* like her mother and who finally, officially, *wasn't*, had told her she'd been named Margaret by her blood mother, she'd nearly laughed at the irony of having two mothers who'd had absolutely no sense of who she was to the point that the first decision each of them had made about her was erroneous: She had been misnamed twice!

Well, she'd show them. Father not her father, but dead anyway when she was twenty-three. First baby dead by the time she was twenty-four, and the topper, at twenty-five: "You're adopted." At the saddest, most bereft time in her life she'd chosen to go for happiness. Upon returning to America she legally changed her name from Phyllis to Felicity.

7

AFTER LUNCH, Felicity does the dishes. "Jesus Christ," she says, scraping food into the already full bag. "Why do I always have to ask you to take the garbage out?" Even as the words leave her mouth she hears how critical she is. The man made lunch for god's sake. Can't she give him a break? After all, she's perfectly capable of throwing it away herself.

"Give it to me," he says, grabbing the bag from her. In an attempt at kindness she kisses the back of his neck as he bends to tie it up, but she still can't believe this is an issue between them. OK, so after years of her teasing him for being garbage-adverse, he'd finally told her that as the eldest of three boys it had been his nightly duty, starting at age eight, to take out the day's garbage, which had entailed going through the basement of the tenement building where his family lived and then out into a dark alley down which he would run in terror to the bins at the far end.

She had empathized with him then, but now it enrages her that he is still procrastinating often for so long that she will give up and do it herself. What is his problem? They are living in the country. There is no dark alley here, merely a pleasant walk through the garden and across the lane to the communal bin.

And what is *her* problem, she wonders, as she watches him walk up the steps to the garden gate? How convenient it is to find fault with him rather than look at her own defects. She can't resist calling after him, "Mind the wild boar don't get you!"

He turns at the gate, grinning at her. "They prefer roots to Jews," he says.

"In that case we're both safe then," she retorts. "I have no roots."

They spend the afternoon at their desks: Spouse going through images of his latest body of work in preparation for an upcoming exhibition, Felicity attempting to write. She loves these afternoons spent in close, silent proximity to each other, each lost in their own work but feeling the companionship. It is, she feels, a perfect example of how a couple can both keep their independence and yet deepen their bond. It is almost as though the bond is the foundation that makes their separateness viable.

It took Felicity a while to get started. She sat for a good half hour feeling dread, uncapping and capping her pen, checking e-mail, ordering something online. It didn't escape her as to how rich it was that she had so recently judged Spouse for procrastination. Finally she reads back over what she already has and it is as though the anger on the page reenergizes her and before she knows it, the afternoon has passed in a nonstop flow of ink.

"Can I interrupt?" Spouse asks. The sound of his voice, gentle as it is, is jarring. She looks up at him as if she's never seen him before. Seeing the look on her face he asks, "Are you all right?" Slowly she reenters reality and finds it both disturbing and a relief. Disturbing because now she exists again, and a relief because she is not alone.

"Why don't you go downstairs and rest for a bit?" Spouse says. "I'll start on dinner."

Once again she is torn; this time between gratitude for his kindness and guilt at her tendency to pick at him. Why can't she just surrender? Why is she still so undeserving?

"It's okay," she says, getting up from her desk. "I can help."

After dinner they take a stroll around the garden. Time is suspended in those few moments between day and night, between sunlight and moonlight, light and dark. Not for the first time Felicity wonders at the calmness that comes with evening, the word itself implying harmony, a lack of competition and imbalance, the gray nonverbal state of merely being.

A memory flashes her back to the years of coke addiction while married to Spouse Number Four. Nights spent snorting and painting alone in her studio. Then it had been the moments before dawn that gave her a sense of well-being; she longed to stay there before the world woke up and made demands of her to which she felt inadequate.

A whisper of air shivers the olive trees. "Look," Spouse says, pointing to the sky. The first star has appeared. A solitary presence in the vast unknown.

8

FELICITY HASN'T SLEPT WELL. Doesn't sleep well anymore, which is something else that pisses her off. All her life she's slept like the proverbial baby no matter what disaster, drama, divorce, death, drugs . . . oh, all right, during her cocaine years she'd have to pop ten milligrams of Valium to fall off the razor's edge into the arms of Morpheus. But really, all her life, no matter what, she'd put her head on the pillow and be gone for eight hours solid. Now, for three years, she's been doing what she calls dolphining: falls asleep quickly but comes to the surface as many as sixteen times a night, as though she needs to grab a mouthful of air before diving back into the depths of dreamland.

It pisses her off because a) she can't figure out why this is happening and b) three years of *dormus interruptus* is, if not actually causing, certainly adding to her daytime irritability. Never known for a long fuse now it is shorter than short and anything could cause combustion. Anything that in any way impedes the rhythm of her efficiency will do it. It could be as mundane as not being able to open the garbage bag quickly enough. Quickly enough for what? To fill it up with more crap? All the crap no longer needed? Old fridge food, labels (labels piss her off too?), peelings, plastic grocery bags, coffee pods, nail trimmings, hair-cuttings . . . fill it up, tie it up, throw it out. Hey, is there room in the bag for a short fuse? Because really, she doesn't want hers anymore.

So why? Why such disturbed sleep? Why, when she's finally living with the man she loves, in a country she loves, free of cigarettes, booze, and drugs for three decades, enjoying a healed relationship with a daughter whom she had thought would judge her until death relieved them both, why, in the tranquil nights of the valley, the night air a cool whisper in the bedroom, spooned into Spouse, why can she no longer sleep well? The more she asks herself this question the more anxious she becomes because she doesn't like that this disturbance began at exactly the same time that she finally got what she'd wanted for forty-five years: to return to living in Europe.

When she wakes up this morning for the umpteenth and final time, she feels, within seconds of consciousness, the shroud of negativity descend. Feels the struggle it will take to lift it, feels exhausted before even getting out of bed. Cramps start in both calves and she stands to attention before they travel upward. She'd rather give birth to a leprous elephant before writhing on the floor with double thigh cramps. She heads them off and falls back onto the mattress, determined to summon the courage to examine the inter—or inner—connection between sleep deprivation and wish fulfillment. Could it be that getting what she wanted is still punishable by death? Could it be that she has become her own watchdog, a one-woman night patrol waking up every twenty minutes to see if she is still alive? Jesus Christ, is life just one big fucking onion with never-ending layers to be peeled? It was enough to make you cry.

9

LIKE MOST LONG-MARRIED COUPLES, they had their routines. Spouse, first into the shower, Felicity to the kitchen; open the curtains to the big glass doors, put the key outside so as not to be locked out. Brilliant idea, that. Couple of thousand years in a culture known for its functional design ingenuity and here we are in the twenty-first century and it would seem that the natives are yet to figure out that you could have both a lock *and* a handle on a door. Not that Felicity has much call to judge, finding herself these days without a handle or a lock on anything.

While Spouse finishes up in the bathroom, Felicity puts out the bowls, plates, mugs, water in the kettle, kettle on simmer, timed to arrive at the perfect temperature for making the morning cup of ginger tea. Oh, how Felicity loves her military precision. Yogurt, fruit, juice, honey, rice cakes, almond butter, all lined up awaiting assemblage by Spouse. Like tennis players switching ends of the court, they pass each other midway between kitchen and bathroom. The routine always the same. Her toilette completed just as Spouse puts the assembled ingredients on the table. And even this early in the day Felicity can feel the tension mounting as she gels her hair, dabs on a bit of make-up, washes her eyeglasses with soap and water, and calls out to Spouse, at that precise moment, every morning, "I'm just thirty seconds away." Spouse, oblivious that for Felicity, being late for anything is close to a punishable crime, calling back to her, "No rush."

So it's interesting that Felicity is willing to take a risk so early this morning. Passing Spouse on her way to the bathroom, she makes a sudden detour, up the stairs to her desk where she googles the meaning and origin of "a short fuse."

It would seem that all dictionaries agree on its meaning, namely to be quick-tempered. All but one. The Urban Dictionary's example of defining a short fuse is enough to make Felicity blow a gasket:

"A woman who achieves orgasm very quickly" (orgasm highlighted in blue, meaning what? Orgasm equals porn?) *"to the point that it can happen accidently."* Are you fucking kidding me? Show me a woman who accidently comes to orgasm quickly. And as if that wasn't laughable enough, this dictionary provides her with an example of a possible plea from this poor woman: *"Please be gentle, I have a short fuse."* What the hell?!

"Listen to this," Felicity calls down to Spouse and repeats what she's just read. Spouse is slicing cherries into their bowls. "I mean what the fuck," she continues. "Who is this woman? And, really? If you make her come accidently she gets pissed off?" Spouse nicks his finger with the paring knife, wishing that he could, just once in his life, have had sex with a woman who came too quickly.

Felicity scrolls down the screen looking for the origin of the phrase and likes what she finds in the British Dictionary:

Origin: 1635–45. Italian. Fuso.

Yes!! Go Italy.

It was one of the things Felicity had loved when she and Spouse first went to Italy in the early nineties: the lack of shame and inhibition when it came to expressing anger. No big deal. Everyone yelled at everyone and then moved on. It had been such a relief to be in a culture unafraid of a short fuse. Felicity has never understood why anger is such a no-no in America while violent rage seems to be just fine. Spouse is terrified of Felicity's anger, shrivels before it, which makes her angrier. Toss it back or laugh it off, she'll say to him, pointing out that her anger has yet to mortally wound him.

She closes the computer and races down to the bathroom aware that she is now behind schedule. Whose schedule, Felicity? Who is demanding that you arrive at table perfectly coiffed and made-up at the exact moment that Spouse puts breakfast before you?

She skips the shampoo goes straight to conditioner, rinses, towels off, the blend of anxiety and anger already mounting in her. So, the thing is, Felicity, why so much anger over such insignificant things? Sure she believes in the relevance of righteous anger, but hasn't she stepped over a line? Not only with regard to the increasing number of things that make her angry, but at the way it sometimes tips toward rage; the flame once lit, racing up the fuse, gaining intensity, aiming to detonate her heart.

10

"HOW ABOUT WE HAVE BREAKFAST OUTSIDE?" Spouse suggests.

"Sounds good," Felicity agrees.

Although it's still spring, the morning is bright with sun, the warmth of which will stay temperate for only a couple of weeks. So Felicity treasures these mornings that allow them to sit on the little terrace around the side of the house, the old wooden table for two nestled next to the pomegranate tree; a tree which, as Felicity has observed more than once, resembles the fifty / fifty nature of life in that in a few weeks it will blush profuse with trumpetlike flowers, yet come autumn will not bear a single fruit. Both Spouse and Felicity look forward to this time of year when the garden is full of bloom and perfume, yet before the arrival of flies. In another couple of weeks the sun will be too hot to sit here and they'll move to the long farm table under the wisteria-draped pergola in front of the house.

As they carry their breakfast trays to the terrace, Spouse marvels aloud at the garden. "Look what you have made," he says, and his joy and admiration melt Felicity's distemper, even as she's already looking for the flaws in her creation. "I mean, really," he continues, "do you have any sense of what you've achieved here?" He stands for a minute still holding his tray. "Just look," he urges. And she does. Three years old this month, the garden looks as if it was always here. Three years of hacking away at stone, planting lavender and roses and beds of succulents, another of gaura. A large raised bed in front of the pergola is rich with thyme, rosemary, oregano, chives, mint, marjoram, parsley, and verbena. Ten big old olives trees dotted around the property had been dug in by a nursery. Hours of bulldozing each hole big enough for their massive root-balls, while Felicity had hacked away with something called a *male-peggio* (bad-worse), a nifty little tool resembling a miniature pick axe. With this she has struck the ground over and over, watching sparks fly as it hit the obdurate flint. And her thumbs have gone from bad to worse with every strike until now there are times when she can barely hold her pen. Her triumph over this ground had, for a while, made up for the lack of triumph in gaining access to the publishing world. How many times has she mused on the irony that on either side of their patch of land lay fertile earth, whereas theirs sits on a vein of rock that runs down from a nearby quarry. If that isn't a metaphor for her lack of gaining entry into the literary world, what is? Obviously she lacks the appropriate tools.

Nor is the irony lost on her that before attacking this particularly impenetrable ground, they had summered on Cape Cod where she had created a garden on sand. On *that* barren patch she had toiled for twelve years, bringing in topsoil, ten varieties of roses, pine trees, tamarisks, and a border of Russian sage alongside Spouse's studio. A miniature dune of sea grass and *rosa rugosa* had created a bit of a barrier from the sea wind and the prying eyes of strollers on the beach in front of them. Folly, the local nursery had told her when she chose a large linden tree to stand beside her tiny writing shed. "A linden tree?" the nursery owner had guffawed. "On the edge of the sea?" But she'd shown him. Two summers she'd spent hosing it down every evening to rid it of the wind's salt deposit, until it found the courage to withstand the assault. What once had been a seedy fence exposing them to the street became, within three years of planting, an eight-foot tall fence of privet; dried blood and manure spread at the roots each spring. If a plant didn't survive a year she yanked it without pity, replacing rose of Sharon, tiger lilies, and butterfly plants with a white tree hydrangea and a border of scarlet Knockout roses. Ornamental grasses grew shoulder high and waved to the sea. Honeysuckle and sweet autumn jasmine vied for space along the fences on each side of the cottage. Into the arched gate, Felicity had carved the legend of Spouse's proposal to her, right there, one Sunday morning and all who entered the gate stopped and gasped at the winding footpath that led to the sea. A triangle of black-eyed Susans and cosmos to the left introduced three triangular raised beds of vegetables, salad greens,and tomatoes. To the right the woodland garden of ferns and hostas, lady's slipper and bleeding hearts led to her shed. The shed, six feet by eight feet, where she had written two of her unpublished novels, had been built with money she'd earned from composing music for a local commercial. The humble structure built by two brothers the day after the twin towers fell. The brothers, Spouse, and Felicity, all in tears as the last nail was driven in, as if this tiny structure bore hope for the future, the courage of it rising up when terror befell. And hadn't she risen up time and again? Hadn't she grown a thing of beauty beside the sea, there where the sand sucked greedily at each watering? Now, here on the mean rock and with dry summers, hasn't she made yet another paradise?

She looks around at it all; the stone steps where there had been only gravel, the camellias, the marble bench under one of the olive trees, the walkway of river pebbles along the Mediterranean border, the old wooden bench under the oak tree. Yes, she is aware of her achievement, proud of it even. But like all achievement it came at a cost. Three years of stubborn will conquering the hostile ground has ruined her hands to the point where a mere ten minutes of weeding will create so much pain she'll not be able to pick up a teapot. Yet how can you explain to the person for whom weeding is a never-ending, boring chore that for her it is a humble meditation; crouching low to the earth, head bent, removing one weed at a time, the mind empty, time irrelevant?

In her forties, in a wooded garden in Kyoto, she had watched a woman on her knees picking pine needles from the fallen leaves. She'd stood there for how long, watching the woman who remained undistracted by her presence, picking needle after needle and placing them in a basket? There in the dappled light of a Japanese autumn, Felicity had understood that there was no greater work than tending the earth. For Felicity, gardening is not about ownership. It's about taking care of a little piece of the planet, of creating a small patch of beauty where none had existed before. It is about acknowledging impermanence and being at peace with it. She knows that once she is gone the garden will eventually disappear. Making a garden is all about accepting mortality, whereas writing is all about achieving immortality. Gardening is the thing Felicity does between novels, or when she is working on one; it is what she does each day, before the laundry, the grocery shopping, before going to her desk.

Even now, as she sits down to eat, she sees a patch of weeds gaining ground in the nearby rose bed. She'll take care of that right after breakfast. To hell with her thumbs. To hell with everyone.

11

BREAKFAST, LUNCH, DINNER, groceries, laundry, gardening, and don't forget to bring in firewood, the evenings are still chilly. Oh, and writing, remember? The thing Felicity has been doing since she was in the nuthouse, age twenty-one. She actually doesn't share that info with many people. Well, let's say she didn't used to. Now she doesn't give a fuck. In fact, now she likes to impart that information to the very people from whom she had previously withheld it. The ones who long ago arrived at the upper echelons of wealth and society. It is especially rewarding to Felicity, for example, to let it drop at a table of art collectors on the eve of one of Spouse's many openings. Oh, yeah, she will say, that was when I was in the nuthouse, and will wait for the inevitable pause of utensils held over fine china. The delicious interruption of genteel blah, blah, blah. The discomfort of the unified downward gaze at slow-cooked salmon on fennel puree. Or, even better, the disconnect between a raised spoonful of lavender panna cotta and the open, filler-plumped lips that await it, lips now agape in the absence of dessert or a response. Someone, once, had been brave enough to fill the silence by asking Felicity how long she had been a psychiatric nurse, to which she had gleefully responded, "Oh, no, I was on the other side of the bars."

Twenty-one, in love with a married man, fired from the Canadian Broadcasting Corporation for being in love with the married man who also worked there; the married man allowed to keep his job and his wife. Felicity out on her ear, somehow managing to get hired as a continuity girl for a soon-to-be famous Hollywood director. Let's rechristen him Robbie Ackerman and let's be honest and say she got the job because she let him go down on her, his tongue being more capable than his dick. And while he might not have been in over his head, she certainly was. Five years since leaving her parents' home, one marriage already failed, Felicity was a walking collection of Band-Aids, stuck on numerous leaks and wounds. Her self-confidence confined to her performance in bed. The confidence needed in order to fulfill her lifelong dream of being an actress completely lacking.

At a cast party, early on in the shoot, Ackerman had called on her to improvise and she froze. He laughed at her before moving on to one of the actresses and as Felicity had sat there she felt herself diminished to risible insignificance, doomed to failure in love and longing. Her heart still aching for the married man, she left the party and walked miles in the dark, over bridges and through unfamiliar neighborhoods, finally remembering the location of her recently rented room.

She has no recollection of how she got them, but swallowed ten Valium and waited until the fear of death outweighed the desire for it. And then she called her ex-boss's wife who came for her, took her to their home, made her cups of black coffee and walked her up and down the hallway until she vomited.

Let's not rechristen that kind soul. Let's call her by her given name: Janet Fox. Angel of mercy. The next morning she asked Felicity if she would like to go to hospital and relief flooded her. Yes. Please. Take me away.

Felicity vaguely remembers Janet taking her to a doctor, the doctor writing a note, Janet driving her to the outskirts of Vancouver and parking outside the tall iron railings. What Felicity remembers vividly is the long gravel driveway that led to the mental institution, the agonizing delay in reaching its doors as Janet bends to retie her shoe, panic rising in Felicity's throat, hurry, hurry, hurry, and the immediate relief as they enter, as if she has finally found home, the doors closing behind her, their barred glass windows emblazoned with the institution's name. *Hollywood Hospital.* I made it, she thinks, as the nurse takes her clothes. I made it to Hollywood.

She is given a bed at the end of the women's ward. A window, situated at the foot of her bed, looks out to an enormous conifer whose presence comforts Felicity; as if something of that girth, of that age, signifies what might be achieved by slow, silent growth.

She is allowed to keep her robe of floor-length crimson velvet that had been made for her honeymoon night, the shade of red an almost exact match with the honeymoon suite's floor-length curtains in front of which she had stood waiting for her new, drunk husband to exit the bathroom, and when he did, had watched him blearily search for her until he finally found her disembodied face amidst the drapery.

She is allowed to keep her make-up, too, and her toothbrush, a gift from the married man the first time they'd spent a dirty weekend together. A novelty toothbrush that when raised to the mouth jingles the opening to "Baa Baa Black Sheep."

She feels no shame. She is home. And, as one can when at home, she quickly establishes a morning routine that will not waiver for the next three months. Up at six o'clock to claim the communal bathroom to herself. The ten-minute soak in the tub followed by a few exercises to keep her pert breasts up where they belonged, the immaculately applied make-up, her bob held back from her forehead with a velvet band. Then to her bed, to the window, to the tree. Her gown arranged just so. "Appearances are everything," her mother used to say, and now Felicity knows they are; they are everything that covers nothing.

12

THAT'S DEFINITELY GOING IN THE NOVEL, Felicity decides as she sips her ginger tea. Spouse is reading something from *The New York Review of Books* on his iPad. Felicity, knowing she's never going to be reviewed anywhere, realizes she's free to say whatever the fuck she wants. Not only on the page but in life. She fantasizes being at the next social gathering. Sees those dessert-laden spoons halfway to mouths and relishes the idea of taking them all behind the bars. Because no one ever asks her to tell them what they'd all love to know. No one asks what was *that* like when she informs well-heeled strangers that she has the unique privilege of being the only one at table who is a certified nut. Not once has anyone overcome fear and embarrassment to engage with Felicity on this subject. Until now, she has watched the paused spoons and open mouths gradually continue their journey toward sugar gratification while desperately thinking of a way to move the conversation elsewhere. Men harrumphing into napkins, the most frightened women excusing themselves for a trip to the powder room. Spouse, caught between admiration and horror, coming to the rescue with a deftly timed question about the validity of Damien Hirst's art. But what everyone *really* wants to know is what it's like "inside." Everyone hopes for a Nurse Ratched, if not the lobotomy.

"I'll tell you what it's like," Felicity will say. It was comforting and frightening. It was clean and orderly. The meals were on time and adequate. The inmates beyond Buddhist. Here was suffering and here was the rant about it. Here was the thrill of exhibition pitted against the rule of authority. Here was the middle-aged woman who came to Felicity's bed in the night. Every night. Her presence waking Felicity up. Felicity looking up into the searching face not twelve inches from her own. Each of them recognizing that neither had what the other needed. Here in bed number eight was the menopausal wife whose husband had elected to eradicate her, signing her up for shock treatment every Tuesday morning until what was left of her brain was incapable of discerning time. So that when the waft of her body odor started permeating the ward a nurse would gently tell her, no, it was not yesterday that she had bathed. It was a week ago. Here was the corridor that separated the men from the women. And here, on the left was the coffee shop, opposite the dispensary. A nifty pairing of venues distributing caffeine and sugar on one side and antidepressants and tranquilizers on the other. This was the luxe area of the institution for those capable of pacing without murder or mayhem. Before you got to the bars. On this side of the bars you could watch the senile judge wheel himself into the coffee shop, order and ingest a coffee and a chocolate donut and then shit himself before turning and wheeling himself away, crying, "Justice," the roll of toilet paper laughably placed on the hand brake, neither of which he ever used.

Her first week inside was a blur. Until it wasn't. She was given drugs that suspended time and agony and a ten-page yes/no questionnaire that she later found out was used to diagnose her. She was, at this point, allowed to make one call per day at the pay phone just a short way down the hall from her ward. The first time she went to make a call she had, by the time she arrived at the phone, absolutely no memory of who it was she'd intended to call. The next day she succeeded in recalling the name and number of the married man. The wife answered. Felicity begged. The wife hurled abuse. Felicity screamed in the hallway. More of a howl than a scream yet blood-curdling even to her. Nurses and a male attendant ran toward her, picked her up, carried her sobbing to her bed, lifted her robe, pulled down her panties, and stuck her in the buttock like an animal. When she came to the next morning it dawned on her that this was a dangerous place. There were rules. And labels. And hierarchy. There was a drug for everything and a place behind the bars waiting like a hungry beast, waiting to devour fragility and turn it into raving lunacy.

Mary, there at the bars every night. Dressed to seduce. Probably sixty. Overweight. A black skirt with a slit up the side. Fur-trimmed slippers, the fur mangy like an alley cat. Mary naked above the waist except for a string of Pop-It beads and misapplied lipstick. Mary, calling through the bars to the male nurse, "Come on, honey. Give Mary a cigarette."

Felicity doesn't remember exactly when she started writing. Maybe the second week? What she remembers is an elegant, older woman in bed number ten. Bea. Her hair always up in a Katherine Hepburn topknot, hands busy knitting, her manner so calm. She looks out for Felicity the way she might have done with the daughter she never had. Felicity is puzzled as to why Bea is there and has no memory of who it was who told her Bea is a chronic alcoholic who is admitted three times a year to be helped through the DTs and the subsequent drying out period. It is Bea whom Felicity first writes about. Then the Judge. And Mary. Eventually she will write about sixteen year-old Gerry. The Philosopher she calls him, and together they pace the hall sharing thoughts and beliefs that only they could understand. They are innocents in the garden of the mad. And then he is gone. Panic in the hall early one morning. His body hanging in the bathroom. The body removed. The hush penetrated only by the whisper of Nurse Janice, the whisper in Felicity's ear, "Schizophrenia."

Schizophrenia. Such a lovely name. Perhaps that of a tragic operatic heroine. Schizophrenia. Mild. The doctor informs her. He's long dead now so let's call him by his name. Dr. Maclean. Owner of Hollywood Hospital. Psychiatrist. Handsome. Like her daddy. She entertains him in his office twice a week. He tells her she is a flower in need of sunlight. But first he looks down at her questionnaire and tells her she is mildly schizophrenic and she is pleased and doubtful. Pleased to finally have a label that explains everything, maybe even lets her off the hook. And doubtful as to the legitimacy of the diagnosis. There had been so many questions that could never be answered with a yes or a no. That was the whole problem with life. It just wouldn't fit into the either/or categories that would make it so much easier to navigate. How many times had she ticked box yes or box no, the way one might pin a tail on a donkey? But never mind. She'd call her big brother later and tell him, almost proudly, where she is and who she is and ask him to tell her parents, whom she doesn't yet know are not her parents, and then perhaps they'll feel sorry for her, maybe even love her. Love her enough to come and get her and take her to the home she's never had.

13

ANOTHER LUNCH COMES AND GOES, followed by their usual espresso with a square of dark sea-salted chocolate. "You must be getting ready to write," Spouse says, as Felicity wipes the last drop of coffee from the little cup with her forefinger.

"Why do you say that?" she asks, not sure if she is happy to be so easily read by the one she loves or irritated that she is such an easy read. Ha, there's a phrase she'd read a few times, countless times actually in over a quarter century's worth of rejection letters. An easy read. Emotionally true. Believable characters. But sorry. Or, just no thanks. Sometimes a glimmer of hope when asked to feel free to submit the next novel.

"I know," Spouse continues, "because your right leg is jiggling nonstop and you have that far away look in your eyes." She laughs and reaches across the table for his hand at the same time that he reaches for hers. "Go up to your desk," he says. "I'll do the dishes."

She sits at the old table that is her desk, its amber wood imbued with the secrets of tales gone by. She loves the company of these spirits, their wordless history ready to absorb her stories. She uncaps her pen, a tiny black Montblanc with a fast, chubby nib. She looks out the huge window that had once been a two-story tall set of wooden doors through which the cows came for shelter on a cold winter night. Back then, before this area had been discovered by the likes of her. The half-loft floor on which her desk sits had been where they kept the hay. Sometimes in the silence of a winter evening, Felicity gets a whiff of the sun-dried grain, can imagine the muffled shuffle of the animals below. On either side of the central section of what is now their home are what had been the living quarters of the peasant families. Now they house Felicity and Spouse's bedroom and bathroom and two guestrooms with their own bathrooms. But back then generations of farmers had lived in these spaces. They who had toiled on the land, mended fences, sharpened blades, chopped wood, slaughtered pigs, and grown all they could eat in the way of vegetables, salad greens, and fruit. The last generation of these people of the land are now in their seventies and eighties, and Felicity and Spouse know they are lucky to witness a way of life that will soon be gone. A way of life dedicated to doing what it takes to survive. Unlike now, when everyone "farms" it out.

There is an old couple up the hill still, along with a brother. These three work slow and steady from dawn to dusk; the olive grove, the wheat fields, the vineyards from which a bottle of red or white wine will cost you all of a euro. Libera's garden, ripe with cucumbers, zucchini, eggplants, lettuce, celery, onions, cabbage, carrots, parsley, all grown from her seeds. Oh, and the plums and apricots, their sun-warmed juice dribbling down your chin. Her tomatoes fill one's dreams all winter. Life here is cyclical and seasonal and basic. One glass fits all. One pair of trousers for the fields, another for Sundays. Everything taken in stride as nature hurls her menu at the land. This year fruit flies, another year aphids. A disease sneaks into the cypress trees. No rain for months shrivels the fruit and grapes and they fall wasted to the ground. A warm spell early in the spring is followed by a frost that kills the tender new leaves on the vines. Hail the size of ping-pong balls bruises grapes right before harvest. Wild boars find a hole in the fence and dig up vegetables and trample fields of ripening wheat. A wolf steals into the sheep pen and rips the lamb out of the ewe's belly. And Felicity loves all of this, this basic struggle for survival. Yes, there are postcard fields of sunflowers whose sun-drenched heads can make you gasp. Morning mists that in winter freeze on bare branches making them tinkle like Venetian glass. The husbandry of the woods, the lumber cut and stacked with precision until each stack becomes a work of art that Andy Goldsworthy would admire. The golden light of a summer evening holding you in its embrace and every face reflecting its grace. The church bells chime; this way for a wedding, that way for a funeral. But the one o'clock chime never changes. Stores shutter, workers lay down their tools, trucks pull into roadside cafes, and wives and mothers everywhere put food on the table. All afternoon the streets are silent. The wicked rest along with the innocent.

This accumulation of time gathering into each moment and every moment that came before, is in sync with Felicity's inner rhythm. Here she feels both calmed down and energized. Is relieved not to measure time as a linear concept. Knows what she has always believed, that time is a man-made construct that cannot be adjusted. Put the clock forward. Put it back. The cuckoo knows. We live in dimensions. We loop back on ourselves hoping to make up for lost time. But time was never ours to lose. And memory is not linear.

Felicity watches the sheep stroll down to the watering hole and then inks the date onto the page as if in defiance. "Oh, I'm not finished yet," she writes. "You haven't been behind the bars yet. You ain't seen nothing until you've been behind the bars."

Nurse Janice had befriended her. Probably just a few years older than Felicity, Nurse Janice was pretty and cheery and a single mother with a little girl. Her left leg was withered from childhood polio but she flaunted her uneven gait, aware perhaps of the sassy sway it gave her right hip. She liked Felicity's hairstyle and Felicity told her she loves to do people's hair. "Perhaps you'll do mine on Friday," Nurse Janice said. "I have a date." And there went that hip.

But first Nurse Janice will tell one of the doctors of Felicity's gift with hair. The next day she's taken behind the bars to the women's cells. The aroma of body excretions and disinfectant makes her gag. But she's on a mission, she's been told. Nurse Janice takes her into a cell on the left where one of the most beautiful women Felicity has ever seen is sitting in the far right corner. There is a cot and just the chair she sits on. She is probably ninety but she is ageless. She is a sprite and a seer. She is the karma of all wild and gentle animals. She is rail thin and lit from within. Her dark, dark eyes a cliché of burning coals in a chiseled face, the beauty of which a web of wrinkles has failed to obliterate.

But it is her hair that takes Felicity's breath away. It would fall to her waist if gravity could tame it. Instead it flies out from her head and shoulders in silver filaments, a tangled growth of energy. It is her pride. It is her mane. It holds the history of her life, her loves and pain and suffering. It could not be equaled on any stage, nor is any brush or comb or human allowed near it. But Felicity is the chosen one. She already has the scissors in her hand. The woman screams and rides her chair further into the corner of her cell and Felicity knows she is the one who will betray her. She waits. Her eyes never leaving the other's eyes. She pours all of her own pain and empathy, her small kernel of wisdom, out into the space between them. "I will not hurt you," she says, even though she and the creature both know that in fact she will deliver the final wound.

They both know there is no choice. If not Felicity, then it will be a needle to the buttock and an electric razor.

Felicity touches the bony shoulder. A tear falls. Slowly, gently, Felicity takes the silver mantle, three feet of knotted tresses falling at their feet. As she whittles it down, Felicity notices the planes of the face, the hairline at the nape, the delicate ears, the catlike chin, and the scissors become a chisel, a little less here, a little more there, the cowlick coiled like a yarmulke, dictating the direction of what is now an inch-long pixie cut capping what once was a wild spirit, now weeping silently in the corner of her cell. She whispers something Felicity cannot hear. And if time can so be measured, it will be sixteen years until Felicity opens her hair salon.

14

FELICITY CAPS HER PEN. Energy is vibrating through her body. Is it the same body that had resided not once, but twice, within the confines of Hollywood Hospital? Surely it is the same energy, the breathless wonder of it, the feeling of reckless rightness. How could you explain the oxymoron of that? How, as a child, could you contain such energy? Exuberance coursing through her back then, exuberance born of the innate knowledge that everything was possible, that the world, that *her* world was a unique place and that she had the right to a place in it. The exuberance always dangerously close to annihilation. The urge to communicate the wonder of it all, until that day in the classroom when the teacher had drawn something on the blackboard and labeled it something, and in that moment Felicity had known with a certainty mixed with terror and thrill that there would never be a way to prove that what all the other students took for granted as a common, identically experienced denominator was in fact an illusion. That just because you drew a table and called it a table didn't guarantee that we all see the same thing. It was that energy that filled her then, an energy born of mystery and the realization, in whatever language an eight year-old child might have, that we are all intrinsically alone and *that* is the only reality we share. And it is that energy that accumulates in Felicity's body when she writes, until it gathers such speed and intensity that she must cap her pen. Or die.

Then she will calm herself by typing the day's ink-fueled pages into her computer; the distance created between the visceral bloodflow of the pen and the cool, touch-typing on the keyboard, allowing her to disconnect, to separate herself from the mad wild ride of creation and become the cool-headed copy editor, correcting and revising as she goes. Once she hits "Save" it is not only the words that are saved, it is her sanity.

How fine is the line between sanity and spirituality? And where is the line between spirituality and superstition, and how can one measure the distance between superstition and extrasensory perception? How can you trust in adults when they tell you one thing, while you, the child, knows that it cannot be true?

And Felicity had known, with perhaps her first complete, conscious thought, at the age of two, while sitting on her potty trying to produce what her mother needed from her, sitting there straining to deliver a fully formed shit for her mother, her mother standing in the doorway like an immense immovable sculpture dressed in her flowered house smock, the one with the red buttons marching up her front, buttons that Felicity tried to count even while lacking that skill. It was when she reached what she saw as the belly button she knew that was not her mother. The mixture of relief and terror pushing the fecal matter out of her tiny body in a bum-splatting rush of diarrhea.

And what does a child do when the truth she knows with her body is denied by the parent? Of course, at two, Felicity had no concept of, well, conception . . . or adoption. All she knew was there had been a terrible mistake and she'd landed in the wrong place. A few years later, when she asked if she was adopted, her mother had laughed at her, told her not to be ridiculous, of course she wasn't adopted. And so had that been the crazy-making moment? Was that when Felicity got the message that whatever she felt, whatever she thought she knew was erroneous, and therefore not only was she crazy but she was not to be trusted?

Felicity looks over to Spouse, who is completely focused on selecting images for an upcoming exhibition. "Would you like a cup of tea?" she asks. But what she really wants to ask is, Can you please stop doing what you are doing? Can you please hold me? Because when the writing is done for the day there is the immediate sense of aloneness. Much like reaching an orgasm via masturbation and then when it's over, you look around and wonder where the fuck everyone went.

"Just a mo," Spouse says, his focus never wavering from the screen. And here is the anger again. The default emotion that overrides disappointment. Such a pathetic child you are, Felicity, go make the tea already. It's not Spouse's fault that your mother was a lying madwoman and your father a handsome coward. Actually what Felicity really wants, perhaps even more than to be held, is to read aloud to Spouse what she has written. To feel him listen raptly even though his genuine praise and the glowing reviews that no one else ever gives will leave her feeling an emptiness filled with resentment.

Why, if he thinks she's such a great writer, does no one else? Is he yet another adult telling her what he thinks it is she wants to hear, or what he wishes to be true? And here is where Felicity's narrative begins to change, because in fact she believes Spouse and she believes she is a good writer. Here is where the old story of being rejected as a baby intersects with being rejected as a writer. So this is what is pissing Felicity off: that it is possible to be an adorable baby and a talented writer and neither fact guarantees that anyone will want you.

15

INSTEAD OF GOING DOWNSTAIRS and making a nice cup of tea, taking it out to the *dondolo*, and letting her wild energy dissipate in the late afternoon air while watching cloud shadows striate the hills, Felicity clicks on NYTimes.com and imbibes the latest toxicity on tap from the Government of the United States of America. It's as if she's looking to keep her anger stoked and for sure she's come to the right place. And as if reading *The New York Times* isn't enough to piss her off, she continues on to *The Guardian*, sandwiching herself between two countries with false democracies.

She slams the computer shut, uncaps her pen, and inks a four-page rant about the state of politics on both sides of the Atlantic. When she's done she feels both high and toxic, a feeling she is familiar with from her booze- and coke-fueled years. She reads over what she's written and knows that if she is ever fortunate enough to get an editor, he or she will want these pages deleted. The rationale being that they will date the novel.

Felicity can imagine the tug-of-war that might ensue between this imaginary editor and herself. Felicity would question why it is not appropriate for a protagonist to opine on current affairs, to name names, to judge politicians for their lies and cowardice. Why, she would want to know, is it okay for the far right to spew their views and beliefs all over the Internet while liberals must tuck their so-called privilege out of sight and shut the fuck up? Can a female protagonist, in this case Felicity, not express her opinion, her horror, her sadness, and, okay, her anger at witnessing this moment in history when politicians and social media platforms spread the lies that the underprivileged so desperately want to be true?

She will want to point out to said editor that while the names might date her novel, it is only the names that change. That it is both shortsighted and without hindsight to think that this moment in history is unique. It has all happened before.

The intensity of her rage frightens Felicity. Surely such toxicity will eventually lead to cancer or a heart attack. And she's pissed at herself for breaking the pact she has with Spouse: that they won't read the news every day; that they would read only the headlines on Sunday. Better to start the day with a Seamus Heaney poem. Better to connect with the mystery and beauty of the world and to feel oneself to be a part of that. Because although it is impossible to separate the personal and the political, one could still choose to seek that which is positive in life.

Even so, while she has much in her life that is positive, Felicity feels she was born out of her time when it comes to getting published. She knows that part of the reason is because she's too old and not famous, because now it was all about sales.

When exactly was editorial authority given over to the sales people?

Oh, Felicity thinks, the editor won't like this rant either. And who could blame her? It can't be easy to be passionate about literature and yet be ruled by the bottom line. Used to be that manuscripts were sent directly to an editor, back in the day when a publishing house believed in a writer, and would be happy with selling three thousand copies. Now you need an agent in order to get to an editor. And if you aren't a celebrity, you'll need to hire a freelance editor to help make your manuscript appealing to an agent, who has to be convinced by the end of the first page that it's solid gold.

No, Felicity will not be silenced. She wants it known, damn it, what it feels like to sit in the office of the editor in chief of a publishing company, watching him clutch her manuscript to his chest like it was his newborn baby as he says, "This is going to be our bestseller of the year." Felicity had levitated all the way home. Finally. Finally, someone believed in her. Finally, she was to be published.

The e-mail from the editor came the next week. "We're so sorry but the sales team said no. We're devastated." *You're* devastated? she had nearly screamed. Instead, she capped her pen and looked out to Central Park where she envisioned herself flying over the tiny balcony, over the treetops, eventually becoming a speck on the horizon. But when she opened the door to the balcony the stench of horse piss and exhaust fumes foretold a hard landing and, really, she'd had all the pain she could bear without subjecting herself to shattering every bone in her body. No. She'd be damned if she'd let the political become that personal.

16

WHY HADN'T SHE GONE and made a cup of tea? Because although when asked Spouse had said, "Just a mo," she knew it was just filler. Knew that he was completely engrossed in what he was doing. That within five seconds of her inviting him for tea it was gone from his mind. So, is that the way it is with you, Felicity, all or nothing? In this case, either Spouse joins you on the divan swing for tea or you stay at your desk and drink in the trash talk of the U.S. administration and, Jesus, if the White House was a bit of an oxymoron when inhabited by the Obamas, now it was an off-color joke. Oh, Felicity, let it go for chrissake. Why can you not give yourself some pleasure? Why are you always waiting for Spouse? Who asked you to? You are not a child, Felicity. No one is forcing you to stay at your desk until you get a passing grade.

Yet here she is, seventy years old, still trying to get a perfect report card. She can't quite sort it all out; where one misconception ends and another begins. Maybe it was that hot day somewhere toward the end of the school year. She was ten, had woken up feeling ill, but there was no pity to be had from her mother. Unbeknownst to Felicity, Mother had an agenda and by god, the child was going to fulfill it.

Every year, the board of education in the town of Bournemouth, population then around a hundred thousand, awarded a handful of students a certificate, each one hand-penned with a monastic border and the town's coat of arms. The certificate stated that the child had, for three years, never been absent or late and had been of good conduct. This then, this achievement by Felicity, was to be the written proof for her mother that in spite of the fact that she had adopted the child of a whore (as unwed mothers of the Forties were then deemed to be) that she, mother superior, had made a silk purse out of a sow's ear. This child, who had been chosen to replace the baby who'd initially been chosen to replace the baby girl who died in utero, the announcements sent to all the relatives telling them that *that* child was born of this mother on March 23, 1946. *That* child, due to appearances, having been returned to the orphanage before adoption was embarked upon. And then Felicity, or Phyllis, or Margaret, or whoever the hell she was, born some months later and having the requisite appearance that might pass for her being their blood offspring, became the child who replaced the child who replaced the child who died in utero. Twice removed, she was taken in by her adoptive parents and in turn, the relatives were taken in by her. But, of course, the mother knew, and was, poor soul, ever after on the lookout for any wayward sign of filth or coarseness, of impertinence or promiscuity. Hence the nose rubbed in the wet knickers; hence the slaps across the face for any hint of backchat; hence the need to call her a liar even when she told the truth, to tell the father of her sins that he might punish her accordingly. Hence the ballet lessons, piano lessons, elocution lessons. She would be made to be the perfect daughter, who would never be able to replace the child who died in utero. And the poor mother, who wanted the perfect daughter, hated this daughter to be in any way perfect, because in the end, she wasn't her daughter and therefore victory could not be claimed. But appearances were everything and so the need for this certificate to be awarded, for the ceremony of the award to be photographed and written up in *The Bournemouth Times*, this was the essential goal toward which Felicity had been headed without knowing it.

So, there was, of course, no way that the ill child could be allowed to stay in bed and nursed back to health by a loving mother. No, the child must not be late, must not be absent, must be of good conduct. And she tries, even when, while being marched to school by the mother, she feels she cannot go on. Weak with fever, her head and body aching, she sits on the curb, her feet mere inches from the passing cars, the mother, who actually isn't her mother, telling her to "Get up, get up, we're going to be late." Not even helping her up from the curb but demanding that she rise up and be of good conduct and thank god for the years of sex and drugs and rock 'n' roll that await. Years of bad conduct, absenteeism, and tardiness released with the aid of alcohol and cocaine. Years of the giant "Fuck you." Years of degradation and failure, rising up and falling flat and moving here and there, this country and that, the jobs, the menial, the flickers of achievement and bursts of potential followed by disgrace and divorce and DTs. The thrill of wild abandon and the agony of being hollow at the core.

But she is one of the chosen on that day in town hall, with just two others. She sees the polished floor, perhaps an oak balcony, shafts of light pouring through the windows. Her school shoes polished by Dad the night before. School dress freshly ironed, its demure hem grazing the tops of her knees. Her hair in two ribboned braids, brushed to a golden gleam that morning. And she's holding the certificate that means everything and nothing and she's still striving for perfect attendance and so she cannot leave her desk while Spouse is still working because the equation is:

work = commitment = success. So, of course Felicity can't go and have a cup of tea on her own. That would be goofing off. And ever since she's been sober Felicity has been aiming for perfect attendance. Good conduct, not so much. But for these intervening sixty years she has never once sat on the curb again. Not with a hangover, not with a broken neck, not with a fractured kneecap or a severed tendon, or the flu or a biopsy or an abscessed tooth or a stillbirth or a loss of custody. There has been no sitting on the curb for Felicity. Get up. Get up. Get up. And Felicity gets up and goes downstairs and makes a cup of tea and takes it out to the canopied divan because fuck Spouse and fuck her mother. She's tired and she wants to sit down.

And the certificate? Never once displayed in her parents' house, it sits now on a shelf in a closet in New York, having been brought back to America some thirty years ago. It had its outing for a while, hanging on the wall of her tiny writing shed, next to her MFA in creative writing diploma, which also now keeps the certificate company on that shelf in New York. "They deserve each other," Felicity thinks as she swings gently in the shade. Two pieces of paper that promised the world and got her nowhere.

Felicity looks out to the hills. A mourning dove coos. She feels the burgeoning growth of the garden. A new lamb cries for its mother and Felicity feels sorry for hers. For both of them. They who had the chance for a daughter but just weren't up to it. For a moment, Felicity feels the freedom of the foundling. She kicks off her shoes and lies full length on the curb.

17

ACTUALLY, FELICITY ENJOYS being on her own. Craves it sometimes, truth be told. Once, back in the mid-aughts, she'd treated herself to three weeks at an inn on the edge of the cliffs above St. Ives in Cornwall. The same inn that would one day become the setting for a future novel. But that is literally another story.

As Felicity swings gently back and forth, she lets herself drift back to that April. She had booked the room with the four-poster bed, overlooking the sea and the distant island of Godrevy. She had packed neither pen nor paints, the intention being to allow herself to just *be* in the place she most loved on Earth. To be. To achieve nothing. To tell no one of her life. To awaken each day absent of agenda.

She had arrived late afternoon, having taken the 10:06 from Paddington. The train journey, also her favorite, appearing in nostalgic flashes out the window between tiny jet-lag catnaps. The sight of an ancient oak sturdily alone in a verdant pasture made her weep.

How could she have lived without this land for so long? Sure, pastoral scenes were intermittently blighted with big-box stores and soul-deadening suburbs and vacant factories, but there was enough left intact of her childhood memories to make her feel she'd come home. The hedgerows, thatched-roofed cottages, ponies peering over fences, here and there a mansion of the mighty, chimneys galore, their manicured green upon green grounds. And then, that eagerly awaited moment when the train runs next to the sea, past Langstone Rock, the red sand of Devon, the melancholy gray sky, all of it filled with memories of Wellington boots and a gabardine raincoat. A flash of her father sitting on the October beach in coat and trilby while eight-year-old Felicity swims and splashes and jumps the chilly waves, teeth chattering as he dries her off. Poor old Daddy. Maybe she'd write about him at some point, but now she's in a hurry to arrive at St. Erth, to lug her suitcase over the bridge to Platform 1 and the toy train to St. Ives. Sitting by the window to catch that first glimpse of the village, its mustard-stained roofs, the stone cottages tumbling down from the moors to the harbor. Will the tide be in or out? No matter, wherever it heaves and swells, it does so in turquoise and teal and navy, silvered here and there by coins of sunlight.

She checked in at the desk and went quickly to her room to unpack so she could take a walk before dinner. She climbed over the stile behind the inn, took the lane that leads to the cliffs, the evening air cool and fresh on her skin. Wildflowers, whose names she could never remember, had begun to decorate the banks and hedgerows, some clinging to cracks in rocks. Stalwarts all. She'd save the big walk for the morrow. Now it was enough to stand at the end of the lane and see the thicket she'd enter, anticipating the Alice in Wonderland feeling it will give her before tumbling her out onto the wild cliffs. The sea, now a gentle *shoosh*, would, when she neared it in the morning, become a percussive crash. A fine drizzle started, more of a salt-laden mist really, but Felicity knew how quickly it could penetrate the outer layers of clothing and so had headed back to the inn.

A fire was already ablaze in the lounge, and for a moment, Felicity was tempted to sit next to it but instead decided to return to her room where she ran a bath in the old claw-foot tub, lit candles, and sinking into the steaming water, gazed out to the fading day, the first lights twinkling on in the village down below. She dried herself, applied oils and creams and make-up, her cropped hair slightly gelled, her clothes bearing the stamp of Manhattan trendy. She mused on how far she'd come since performing her morning toilette in Hollywood Hospital. Was she really so different now? Not so frightened perhaps, her poise no longer a posture. Her shyness balanced by the proof of her years; here was a woman who'd seen a thing or two and survived to tell the tale.

As Felicity was shown to her window table at the far end of the inn's restaurant, she felt something to be amiss. There were already a few diners seated at nearby tables, all of them couples. The women eyed her as women will eye another who is single and still attractive. The men, not so much, age being a bigger issue for them. As she unfurled her napkin and looked around the room, she understood that she was facing the wrong way. Some well-meaning, or nosy person was bound to make eye contact, greet her, try to initiate conversation. It would be all the usual questions, and for the first time in her life Felicity did not want to answer them. She didn't want to be known. And more than anything she didn't want to hear her own damn story. She was there to try living in the moment.

She got up from the table and with a simple, gracefully executed move, placed her chair on the other side so that her back was to the room. The lighthouse on Godrevy winked as if in collusion. And for the next three weeks, apart from vocalizing her food order, the only words she uttered were, "good morning," "good evening," "please," and "thank you." She asked no one how they were nor did she tell them to have a good day. No longer a drinker, she knew she could dine early and retire to the lounge with her chamomile tea where, alone in a wingback, she could lose herself to the scenic flames of the fire. She felt herself to be the mystery woman in an Agatha Christie novel and mused on what a great setting the inn would make for a novel, if one could just find a way to trap a handful of characters in this very room and have them go at one another.

Alert to the sounds of the dining room, she heard the first scrape of a chair pushing back from its table, and replacing her cup in its saucer had quietly left the lounge before anyone else entered it. She relished her hushed ascent on the carpeted stairs, the click of the door behind her, the sea a dark beast devoid of slumber, its prowl comfortably at bay, herself silent between the sheets.

For three weeks Felicity accomplished nothing. She walked for hours on the cliffs, strolled the village for candles, a little *pressé*, and some good ground coffee. Several days in a row the rain was too heavy for walks and so she sat in silence at Tate St. Ives, communing with a Mark Rothko canvas, feeling the layers of colors rise up through themselves, feeling the prayerful, manic energy vibrate in her, yet refusing to interpret what she saw. Just as she refused to interpret or transform or relate anything of what she saw and felt during those weeks. For three weeks Felicity experienced the exhilaration and loneliness of merely being. Felt the mystery with no need to explain it.

One day, she climbed down the side of a cliff to the ledge where she hoped one day to be scattered and watched birds fly beneath her. Waves that were a moment ago part of the uncontainable sea were now forced into the confines of the cove where they released their fury against the rocks, and, in that moment, she saw that she had lived her life on a tightrope. The rope originated with her, spinning out from her belly into infinity, a narrow umbilicus upon which she had balanced her life. As in a vision, she had seen herself swivel on the rope and return to a platform where she sat dangling her feet and from that perch had viewed the landscape of her life spread before her, its vast terrain a wonder to behold.

18

"AH, THERE YOU ARE!" Spouse exclaims as if finding her where they live is an anomaly.

"Ha!" Felicity drawls. "And I didn't even have to put a red carnation between my teeth." She curls up her legs, making room for him to join her on the swing.

"Whatchya up to?" he asks.

"Thinking."

"Do I get any clues?"

"Nothing beginning with you?" she says, poking him in the ribs with a bare foot. "What have you been up to?" she asks, in an attempt at kindness.

"Oh, you know, just catching up on some e-mails. Sent some images off to the publisher." And before the word "publisher" has completely left his mouth she sees his anxiety. She knows he is aware of how his success in the publishing world is one grain of salt after another in Felicity's wound of rejection, a wound that seems to come unstitched from time to time. She could imagine him envisioning it as a gaping hole continually emitting a low moan, and knew it freaked him out.

"I'm sorry," he mutters.

"Oh, for chrissakes, don't go there," Felicity says. "It's really not all about you. I am actually capable of holding more than one emotion at a time. Just because I resent not having the success you have doesn't mean I'm not happy for you that you do. Besides, imagine what it would be like if there were two of us moping about unwanted."

"Yes, I know," he says, "but I still feel the burden of having what you don't."

"Oh, spare me," Felicity sits up and reaches for her drink, amazed that it contains no alcohol. "You're just digging yourself in deeper with that false modesty crap, mister. Frankly, it's insulting and disingenuous, and who the fuck cares."

"Ok, well, moving right along," Spouse says and reaches for Felicity's feet, cupping them in his lap, the comfort of his elegant hands always a balm. "Do you want to read me what you wrote today?" he asks. Her heart leaps. She is like a child being asked to pirouette for Daddy. And suddenly her ire and resentment are gone and she is in the warm nest of gratitude. Here is her faithful listener, her eager reader. Here is the one person in the world who gets her, who believes in her, who thinks she is an amazing writer, who marvels at her ability to mold language into provocative, believable narratives. If it weren't for him, she would drown in her own failure.

And yet, as she reads the last chapter to him, she becomes acutely aware of the absolute contentment of solitude that she had felt during those three weeks in St. Ives. Those weeks had not only been about letting go of achievement, they had also been about feeling complete in her aloneness. Had she even missed him? She can't remember. She had been glad to see him upon her return to

New York, that she knew; knew that then, and now, and always, to see him again after any time apart was to see him as she had the first time, with all the wonder and thrill and breathtaking glee that this was her soulmate.

What Felicity couldn't understand, or get past, was how, unlike in the early years, that intense joy at reuniting was no longer followed by languorous kissing, busy hands and the deeper pleasuring of each other. And, as she puts down the manuscript, she wonders if perhaps she would have been more successful without him, or any man for that matter.

She is suddenly appalled to find herself guilty of the thing she always accuses him of: the belief that one can't have both a meaningful marriage and a successful career. How ironic, she thinks, for once not listening to his feedback about what she's written. All the years that she accused him of staying in his first loveless marriage because it allowed him to put all his passion into his art. And what had she been doing all her life? She'd had to be an alcoholic in order to put her art before husbands and, shamefully, her child.

As a sober person, these last twenty-eight years, she has been at a complete loss to find the balance between doing what it takes to grow a marriage and having the courage, or the trust perhaps, to go about her business, her art. Was this really the clichéd lot of wives and mothers who were also artists? This continual tearing away from one thing to fulfill the urge for another? Had she perhaps lacked the urge to be a parent, different in her mind than the urge to be a mother, which she had most definitely felt? Surely the urge to be a mother is biologically instinctive for many women. But does one really, truthfully, have the urge to be a parent with all the nonstop responsibility that entails? Is that why she had abandoned her responsibility when her child was young? Because the urge to create and the urge for a man drained her of the energy required to parent? What the hell? Is the chapter she just read a glittering jewel of revelation sitting on her opened palm? The revelation being that she had been at her most content, had felt most herself when for three weeks she was not a spouse, nor a parent or an artist? Was this why she hadn't been able to maintain that sense of well-being once she stepped back into her life as a wife, mother, and writer, because she had no bloody idea how to prioritize from moment to moment? Is this why she's so fucking angry . . . because she's continually tearing herself from one thing to the next to the next in a never-ending cycle of desire and guilt.

Spouse is talking, what's he saying? "Maybe you should take time out like that more often," he says. And she looks at him, stupefied. She feels disoriented, almost vertiginous, is trying to right herself. What is he saying? That that's allowed? Time to oneself, for oneself? "Really," Spouse says, stroking her feet again. "You're allowed to sit on the curb."

19

FELICITY LOOKS AT SPOUSE, and much like when she once had the vision of a tightrope stretching before her upon which she had precariously balanced her life, she now sees a row of ducks popping up as in a shooting gallery at the carnival. Spouses One through Five, ducks sailing by and disappearing behind cardboard scenery. Each of them had been targets she'd taken aim at and missed, until Number Five. The target really having always been love and loyalty. Strange that her vision, when it came to selecting a lifetime mate, had gotten better with age.

She lies back on the swing, closes her eyes, and watches as the ducks round the backdrop and parade in front of her again, each comically alike, each completely unaware. Of course, in reality, while they might all have been sitting ducks, they each had been lame in their own way.

Spouse Number One had entered her life shortly after she'd arrived in Vancouver at the age of nineteen. It was his tie that did it. She didn't even know she was homesick until she saw it. Didn't know much of anything really. At that point in her life she pretty much went where there was either the promise of love or a job, or a room to rent. How incredibly ill-equipped she'd been for any of the things she undertook. How impossibly young and stupid, and yes, a little brave. In those days, when she wasn't crying or stuffing herself with sugar to mollify the impending scream for help, she experienced herself as always moving toward something, as opposed to fleeing something. It seemed the positive choice, the most hopeful. To run to London at sixteen and the promise of unimaginable success as opposed to acknowledging the pain of life with her parents. Those misbegotten people whom she knew, without the ability to articulate it, had always disapproved of her.

It would seem that Felicity had always been in possession of two opposing streams of energy: the one, forward-moving with an unerring instinct for survival and the other, self-sabotaging, activated as soon as she entered the zone of achieving what it was she wanted, of getting where she wanted to go. I mean, really, Felicity, why Vancouver in 1966? After nearly four years of London. To actually be living in London in the sixties and to be aware, no less, that it was *the* happening place to be, and then suddenly off to Vancouver, dressed in her Mary Quant outfit, still carrying the cheap blue suitcase. From swinging, sexy London to puritanical, suburban Vancouver. What the fuck? The biggest shock had been the lack of humor. But what had been most unsettling was the gridlike design of the city, with streets that went on forever in a straight line, addresses bearing numbers in the thousands, the buildings indistinguishable facades that even the startling beauty of the Rockies and the Pacific Ocean could not ameliorate.

She had originally been offered accommodation in the parental home of her Canadian girlfriend, Maria, a friend with whom she had hitched around Europe the previous summer and with whom she had shared a bedsit in Putney. But the accommodation had been withdrawn at the last minute when a posse of young Aussie men, one of them the ex-boyfriend of Felicity's and all of them friends of hers and Maria's, had gotten there first, so to speak. Arriving in Vancouver two weeks before Felicity, they had been invited to dinner at Maria's mum and dad's and the lads had generously offered after-dinner entertainment in the form of a slideshow documenting their two years of travel around Britain and Europe. And so it was that Felicity showed up stark naked on the screen to a chorus of "Aw, yeah mate, there's The Blonde." Maria having previously sent photos of herself and The Blonde to her parents so there was no mistaking her identity. Evidently, there was a bit of an uncomfortable hush in the den of Maria's parents' house before the carousel clicked on to slides of a bullfight. By the time the letter of disinvitation arrived, Felicity was already packed, notice given at her latest job, plane ticket in hand, courtesy of the Canadian government. The ex-boyfriend had at least the decency to send Felicity the address of three young women who had a room to rent in their house, ironically not far from Hollywood Hospital. So Felicity had found herself in the basement of something called a split-level ranch house, and there, for a month of lonely days without work or money or the courage to venture outside, she had discovered Wonder Bread and peanut butter and something called a broiler and thus spent her days toasting and spreading and eating, fascinated by the way in which something could be so airily empty and yet so intriguingly addictive, as if she were eating her life.

And then, toward the end of that first month, her housemates, such as they were, threw a party and somewhere toward midnight a twenty-two-year-old man came in the door. Newly returned from his own trip around Europe and a sojourn in London, he sported a Beatles haircut, a mod suit, and Chelsea boots. But it was the tie that did it. A colorful strip of flowers, pop-art style, perfectly knotted and yet full of wild energy, it was like the flag of her homeland, the hip, revolutionary city in which she had so recently danced. The tie seemed to vibrate off him, as though his heart was pulsing in the center of every flower. She can still see it, that scrap of material that represented all that she'd left behind, all that she—until that moment—hadn't known she missed. It was as though suddenly a lifeline had been tossed into the waters of the party and she swam toward it, instantly in love.

So it was shocking when, less than a year later, while she and Spouse Number One were exchanging their "I do's" that a thought entered her mind so clearly that for a moment she wondered if she'd uttered it aloud. The thought was "Well, I can always get divorced." Looking back on that moment now, Felicity wonders at how her then-twenty-year-old consciousness was able to skip over the sudden and surely painful realization that this was not the man she wanted to marry and go directly to the inevitable solution. And how had she not known this sooner? Well, it was simple. He had been deeply in love with her and he and his family had taken her in those first few months of life in Vancouver, when, shortly after meeting him, she came down with mononucleosis. They had taken her to doctors and nursed her back to health, so how could she not reward the man? Her first marriage had been founded on the repayment of her indebtedness to his kindness, the likes of which she'd never known before.

Her parents, back in England, had refused to give the consent to marry under the age of twenty-one, the consent necessary under Canadian law. At the time, their refusal was just more proof to Felicity of her parents' continuing need to deny her love. And so it was that she and Spouse Number One-to-be had skipped engagement and gone straight to elopement over the Canadian border to a town called Blaine in the state of Washington. But not before Felicity had shopped for a white lace mini-dress. They were to marry on Christmas Eve and she had spent days looking through pattern books before choosing a Jackie Kennedy–type coat that had then been sewn up by a friend of her soon-to-be mother-in-law. She chose a mauve bouclé and had satin shoes dyed to match. A hairdresser friend had done her waist-length hair; an up-do of carefully pinned coils and curls, each studded with a tiny red rosebud. It was in this bridal outfit that she was rolled up in a piece of carpet and placed on the backseat floor of the best man's Oldsmobile, tucked under Spouse Number One's feet, her bridesmaid in the front seat next to the best man who drove them through passport control and on to the justice of the peace who, along with his snow-white toy poodle, pronounced them man and wife at the exact moment that Felicity was flooded with relief, knowing that she could always get divorced. Which she would be, some eighteen months later, while an inmate at Hollywood Hospital.

Felicity had recently tried googling Spouse Number One in the hopes that she could find him and make amends. For although he had, shortly after their wedding, become a belligerent drinker and lousy lover, who was to say that it wasn't she who had inflicted the first wound? And how had he gone from being her savior to being someone from whom she wished to be rescued? And how incredibly poignant that it had been his mother who set her free. That sweet, pretty woman, mother of five and already a grandmother in her late forties. What was her name? How could she have forgotten her name? Was it Rose? Or was that a different mother-in-law? But surely it must have been Rose, for the woman was love itself.

Felicity could see her now, having invited Felicity to tea one afternoon. It was the summer following the elopement and she can still see her mother-in-law and father-in-law on that icy Christmas Eve, standing on the steps of their tiny house, the house gaily decorated with Christmas lights, as were all the other houses on their street. The parents waiting for the young sweethearts, along with a houseful of friends and neighbors. The generosity of those working-class people enough to make Felicity weep this very minute. Had she known then, the mother? How did she know? Felicity would find out over that cup of tea in the back garden when the petite, pretty woman who is her mother-in-law asks Felicity simply, "Do you love Roddy?" And Felicity looks down in shame and says, "I don't know." And Rose says, "If you loved him you would know." Felicity knew it was that simple even before Rose goes on to say, "There are times when I can't stand my husband, but I always know I love him."

Felicity left the house of the only family she'd ever known. Knew she would never see them again. Knew that an act of loving kindness had been bestowed on her even as the mother's heart broke for her son. And as she wandered the sunny suburban streets, Felicity felt the price of freedom to be very steep indeed.

20

FELICITY OPENS HER EYES and sees Spouse still sitting here, reading something on his iPad, her feet still in his lap. He must think she's dozed off. She closes her eyes again, let him continue to think that. She's not in the mood to tell him what she's thinking or feeling. What *is* she feeling anyway? Angry. Natch. Now what? Angry she hadn't been able to find Spouse Number One on the Internet? Or angry because she feels she's been fooling herself all her life and this particular memory is just one small, unshining example of her desperate need not just for love, but for recognition. And this, she thinks, is the dangerous game she's playing now. Because she knows that to write of her life and have *that* rejected will be the end of her. For if there is one thing Felicity learned early in her "career" as a writer, it is that not everything that's true is necessarily believable on the page. So, why on Earth would she want to put her whole life on the page and either have it rejected by the publishing world, or, even worse, get it published only to have some asshole critic say it lacked believability, that nothing rang true, or perhaps, even though called a novel, that it was a self-indulgent attempt at the memoir.

Believability runs parallel to belonging for Felicity, for if one tells the truth and isn't believed, how can one belong in one's own life?

How many times has Felicity told the truth and been called a liar? What was it with her? Has she in some way fictionalized the truth to herself? Is that what we're doing when we tell stories that we think are memories? And if so much of Felicity's life seems unbelievable to her, why would it ring true to someone else? It's why she's chosen never to write a memoir in spite of friends and Spouse, and even her therapist, urging her to do so. It makes her angry to even think about it. Isn't it enough to have lived through all the dramas without having to write about them? Oh no, she always says, in mock horror at the suggestion; my life would read like one of those trashy novels you pick up at the supermarket checkout, nobody would believe it, she says. Hadn't she had proof that day in college when it was her turn for the short story she'd submitted to be critiqued in workshop?

She can see them now, all those students, some of them the graduating stars of the creative writing program. Some of them already lined up with an agent. The teacher a renowned short-story writer. The story Felicity had submitted was her attempt to fictionalize something that happened to her in early sobriety.

Living alone with her then teenage daughter who that night was on a sleepover, Felicity had just gotten into bed when she heard a voice yelling something in the street below her window. The street being Main Street of a small upstate New York town. A riverfront town that had been making a comeback for a decade without ever actually making it all the way back. Felicity had bought a small eyebrow colonial there, just two months earlier. The down payment of forty thousand dollars being the amount that Spouse Number Four had begrudgingly paid her at the time of their divorce. An amount that, by the way, was a quarter of what the lawyer had advised her to ask for as her due for seven years of marriage and step-motherhood. Ever the sucker, and let's be honest, Felicity, still having the desperate need to be liked, even by a husband who slept not only with almost anything in a skirt, but also with Felicity's lawyer friend whom she had first hired to negotiate the divorce, the two of them actually fucking each other during said negotiations.

But Felicity digresses, so back to the story, which she entitled "Lullaby on Main Street."

On opening her bedroom window to the chilly April air in order to better hear what is being announced on the street, she is astounded to hear the drunken proclamation, "She's having the baby, she's having the baby." The voice belongs to one of the siblings of a local family that, to Felicity's mind, is right out of *Deliverance*, which, if that title had not already been used, would have been the perfect one for this story. One of the brothers is reportedly in jail for attempted murder. Another has a steel plate in his head, having been the victim of the axe-wielding brother. Yet another brother delights in sitting on his balcony, directly across from Felicity's bedroom window, from where he can, with a bottle of something at his side, shoot birds as they land on the power line. Below him lives the sister of the drunken sister now yelling in the street.

For several weeks, Felicity has been watching, in utter fascination, the comings and goings of the downstairs sister. What particularly fascinates Felicity, especially as a newly clean and sober person herself, is watching this obviously pregnant woman seeing her two young daughters off to school each morning. The children are dressed immaculately, their hair neatly braided, the mother hugging them to her before putting them on the school bus, waving goodbye with a cigarette in one hand and a beer can in the other. What moves Felicity is that the power of love is such that in spite of the woman's obvious addictions whatever small part of her that remains intact is the maternal.

It is nearly midnight when the pronouncement of imminent birth reaches Felicity. What to do? She dons the only nightgown she owns, shoves her feet into the nearest pair of shoes, and, grabbing her house keys, runs across the street to the storefront that is this family's welfare housing.

She will never erase the image that greets her. A bed takes up half the room and on it is the naked mother. The eldest daughter is standing at the head of the bed shaking. The youngest is at the foot of it, mouth agape as if watching a cartoon. And what a fucking cartoon it is. The woman is crowning for god's sake. Oh, no, Felicity thinks, that can't be right, and turns to head back out the door as though if she can just reach the safety of her own door the nightmare will end. But of course it isn't a nightmare. And so she turns back to the bed. She takes the children and puts them in the bathroom. She tells them it's all going to be OK. The drunk sister is now hovering outside the door. Felicity tells her to call for an ambulance and then Felicity climbs onto the bed. She kneels between the woman's legs, tells her to push. The woman looks at her but doesn't see her. "Push," Felicity yells, pressing down on the belly. Nothing. Felicity rolls up her sleeves. The baby's head has retreated, as if deciding against entry into such a world. Felicity puts both hands into the woman's vagina. In her memory it will feel as though she was in up to her elbows. She clasps the baby's head in both hands and gently eases it out, its little body slipping silently into the night. It is very quiet. Felicity thinks this is not normal. Any baby in its right mind screams in utter protest at the blaringly cruel exposure to planet Earth. But this little girl is too meek to inherit the Earth. And Felicity is terrified of the cord. Unable to sever baby from mother, she curls herself up into the fetal position between the mother's legs and folds the baby into her nightgown, massaging it and cooing to it; if necessary, she will lick her into being. The baby stirs. She whimpers. And suddenly the street is filled with sirens and flashing lights. The sister, as drunks are wont to do, has called every emergency service, and the room fills up with firemen and police and, thankfully, paramedics. If the image that had greeted Felicity some fifteen minutes earlier was out of a B movie, she cannot begin to imagine what these men think when they see Felicity in a bloodstained plaid flannel nightshirt curled up between a naked woman's thighs, cradling an infant, and calling out in desperation, "I don't know what to do with the cord!"

Someone takes the baby from her. She goes to the sink to wash her hands. The sink is piled with filthy pots and pans and dishes. Felicity would *really* like a drink. She can't find her keys. She hears a voice say, "I just got sober," and realizes it's hers. A paramedic removes her keys from under the naked woman and gives them to Felicity. "Look at me," he says. "I'm sober, too." Felicity walks across the street, lets herself into the only home she's ever owned. She grabs a coat from the hallstand, throws her nightshirt in the garbage, scrubs her hands at the kitchen sink and puts the kettle up for tea.

One of the stars of the creative writing program gives her verdict. "I just didn't find it believable," she says.

"Me neither," says another.

And Felicity thinks, "Fucking story of my life."

21

FELICITY LETS OUT A SNORT, startling Spouse who looks up from his iPad. "You've had a nice nap," he says. Felicity thinks, let sleeping dogs lie. "Do you fancy a nibble?" he asks, closing the device. And not for the first time Felicity thinks how impossible it is for men to be direct. Surely it is *he* who wants the nibble. Why not just say, "I'm gonna get something to munch on, do you want something too?" For fuck's sake, Felicity, build a case, why don't you?

"Why do you do that?" she says.

"Do what?"

"Ask me if I want something as if I'm your first concern, when it's actually you who wants something?"

"Jesus Christ, I can't do anything right these days. It was just a simple question. Sorry I asked." He gets up from the swing and starts heading toward the house.

"Walk away, why don't you?" Felicity calls after him. Typical. Confront a man about anything and if he hasn't got a satisfactory answer or the balls to be honest, then the solution is just walk away.

He turns suddenly and Felicity can see he has on what she calls his rat face. "You've been on my case for days," he says through bared teeth. "I say the simplest thing and you're right down my throat. What exactly is your fucking problem? Because whatever it is I'm sick of it being my fault."

This is a man who doesn't like anger, particularly Felicity's, and he rarely gets angry himself. Which of course pisses Felicity off. She's seen him angry perhaps six times in twenty-seven years. It isn't pretty, although it is slightly thrilling and in the early days had always led to good sex. But today it doesn't seem like much fun because she knows that her lashing out at the man is completely out of proportion to the crime, if indeed asking someone if they'd like a snack can even be called a crime.

"I'm sorry," she says, patting the cushion next to her. "Come back, please." She watches as he considers which way he wants to go with this because, and she knows he'd never admit it, but in the end he is no different than anyone; the energy anger packs is not easily mollified, doesn't like to be interrupted with kindness. Like a lit fuse it wants to run its destructive course until it demolishes its target before fizzling out. To be interrupted mid-eruption is galling, as Felicity well knows.

"I'm sorry," she says again as he sits down. The rat face has softened but he'll be damned if he'll go quietly. His lips remain in a grim line, the eyebrows arched in cold remove. Refusing to look at her he stares into the distance.

Felicity feels tears gathering but thinks they'll be read as manipulative so shoves them back in their sockets. "I just feel angry all the time," she says. "I mean, more than usual. I don't know what's going on. I'm trying to understand it. I know I have everything to be happy for and it's not that I don't feel happy sometimes. Or grateful, a lot of the time. But Jesus Christ, I'm seventy fucking years old and what have I got to show for it?"

He starts to say something.

"No, don't," she says, "I don't want you to make it all better, you can't anyway and besides it's not your job." He reaches for her feet, but she withdraws them, not even able to allow for that small comfort. She's trapped. She wants to be comforted but feels she doesn't deserve it. Or feels it will distract her from her mission. But what is your mission, Felicity? To shift something deep within. Some awful tumor, growing fat on bitterness. Not shift it. Shatter it.

"I'm frightened," she says, and again he reaches for her and again she says no. "No, I have to figure this out myself. I don't want to grow old like this, feeling like a failure. How can people say they have no regrets? I mean, really, is there nothing you regret?

"That's rhetorical at the moment," she says, seeing him about to come up with an answer. "It's not like I haven't known success," she continues. "I mean, I know I was only a big fish in a little pond, but I liked it. It fit me well. I liked having a successful salon. I liked being told fifteen times a day how fantastic I was. I liked that people bought my art; that I was shown in local galleries. I liked that people recognized my voice from the radio. And once I got sober, I liked it all even more. I wasn't actually craving more. Oh, well, yes, I wanted to find the love of my life, but I wasn't looking to be famous. Not in the modern sense. And then, *boom*. Some fucker breaks my neck and that's that."

"Yes, but look at all you've accomplished since then," Spouse says. "Not only did you recover from that horrendous accident but you went and got a degree."

"Oh, right," she interrupts. "That turned out to be of great value, didn't it? What bloody use is a degree in writing? I couldn't even get a job teaching in a jail! By the time I graduated, everyone and their friggin' dog was a writer."

"Yes, but . . ." Spouse starts to say.

"No, there is no but," Felicity yells. "There are only four novels, a play, a book of essays, and a collection of stories, all rejected. What the fuck do I think I've been doing all these years? I've been fooling myself, that's what. I listened to you and everyone else and believed you all. I believed that if I stuck with it, eventually I'd be successful. What a joke. No, what I've really been doing is creating shit no one wants. I'm pissed off because it would seem that rejection is the only identity I think I deserve. And now I'm old and bitter and a failure and it all feels too late. Like I've written myself into a corner. Well, fuck that." She gets up from the swing, turns to Spouse. "I would love a nibble. Do you think you could bring it up to my desk?"

22

FELICITY SITS AT HER DESK, uncaps her pen, and writes "Chapter 22" and stops. What is she trying to say? Not just now, in this minute, but altogether? What is this thing she's writing? Novel? Memoir? Primal scream? Self-indulgent moan? She feels she's lost sight of the beginning, of what impelled her to begin. Anger. Fury. Rage. Some deep urge to let everyone have it, whoever everyone was. How long has it been since someone else's novel had enraged her and what exactly about that novel had ticked her off?

Felicity sits, pen poised, brain fuddled. Anger seems so far away, replaced now by fear and sadness, those inconvenient feelings that anger is so quick to mask. Better to feel the power of fury than the paralysis of fear or sadness.

So, what are you afraid of, Felicity? What was so frightening about the novel that you had to get far away from it as quickly as possible, and did so with those tricky, rubber-handled tools of judgment and anger? It had been the author's tone of complaint, the description of ailing body parts, a creep of decrepitude, and the hint of resignation to come. That's what scares Felicity. She doesn't want to become resigned. It terrifies her. Surrender, that was different somehow. It lacked bitterness and leaned more toward acceptance. Resignation was like a letter to self, terminating one's employment of capability, of courage, of belief, goddamn it; belief that it was never too late . . . for what?

Success, of course. Never too late for success. The old haunting. What the aging characters and, let's be honest, the aging author, seemed to be implying was that success was, in the end, never enough. Isn't that what Felicity is struggling with? The struggle to accept that no matter what, nothing will ever be enough? What was frightening Felicity, hidden beneath her anger, was the fact that the other writer's novel had held no struggle. The protagonist had merely put down her end of the rope. Now *that* was really scary. *Rage, rage, against the dying of the light*. And there's the sadness. It is, at seventy, no longer the light at the end of the tunnel. It is just the end of the tunnel.

Is it normal to feel the nearness of the dying of the light at her age? Is she living her age or that of her seventy-nine-year-old spouse? Damn right, she's afraid. Not of dying . . . she'd been close a couple of times and has tasted the possibility of peaceful surrender. No, what frightens Felicity is the accruing regret she feels at having failed herself and that it *is* too late to rectify that; that once again she is to blame, and as she inks the word "blame" onto the page, a thousand "should"s burst forth like startled birds shot out of a tree. She should have had more courage. She should have gone for what she'd wanted. She should have submitted that application to the Royal Academy of Dramatic Art. RADA or nada. She'd chosen nada. Filled in the form, seventeen years old, alone in a bedsit in Earls Court. Never mailed it. Instead, she'd caved to insecurity, to the vision of embarrassing herself before jurors. Had caved to the fear of ridicule and rejection, already rutted into the groove of that misconception.

Instead, she'd taken her auditions in the beds of men she hardly knew, performing like a star, her streaky blond hair, tousled and tossed on rarely washed pillowcases, her then lovely young body giving it everything she had in the hopes of an encore. When it came to her physicality, she had no doubt of her talent; dancing, fucking, running with the hockey ball down the left wing, shooting the netball right into the hoop, swimming for a win, leaping from rock to rock, cycling downhill no hands. And she's had a good long innings. Even after she broke her neck she was still a hot number. And strong. And, yes, courageous even. Wasn't it she, trapped inside a Halo-Vest, its metal rods drilled into her head, the rods attached to a metal vest immobilizing her from the waist up while C4 through C7 healed in their fusion with the dead man's rib? Wasn't it she who thus attired had urged Spouse Number Five—to-be—to make love with abandon? "It's all good from the waist down," she laughed as she saw the shock on his face. "Think of it as a fancy lobster pot," she'd said, when he'd looked fearfully at the metal contraption. And even though when she'd come home from the hospital with her arms still partially paralyzed to the point where she couldn't feed herself, had she not arisen at six that next morning in order to make porridge for her then seventeen-year-old daughter? Struggling for an hour with arms she could barely lift or control, in order to put some semblance of normalcy in front of her. Oh, sweet, scared daughter.

So love comes into it after all, Felicity thinks, the pen pausing for breath. Courage and love, the courage to love, yes, she had that. Still does. And is this why she now feels so sad? Sitting here now, reading over the last few chapters, the sadness of all that is lost, every day, now and then? Back then, in that first marriage and the mental home. Did she ever drink the tea Rose had poured, or had she left before either of them spilled tears? Had she been an angry person then? No, not really. No, she had to become alcoholic and drug addicted in order to locate that repressed emotion. The beast that had remained in its cave for years would need a large intake of spirits before it could be let loose.

And let loose it is, on a San Francisco bus. The first bus that comes along outside the courthouse where she has just lost custody of her three-year-old daughter. Felicity listening as the inexperienced young lawyer apologizes. There is a fountain splashing somewhere. The lawyer's hand on her shoulder and then she is alone, wailing and walking on disappeared legs. Faster. Faster. She needs to go faster. Get away. Run. Run for the bus. The driver looks at her and looks away. She sits in a side seat, all tears and snot and unspeakable anguish. Passengers look away. Except for one. One passenger looks at her in obvious amazement, and years of injustice and rage rip out of Felicity, "What the fuck are you looking at?" she screams at the passenger and rides the bus to nowhere.

Pen in hand, Felicity sits at her desk. She looks up but sees nothing. Numb? In shock? It's all right while the ink is flowing; somehow the act of actually committing a memory like that to paper, the actual act of that is, yes, okay, somewhat cathartic. But when the pen stops, when the ink no longer flows, then something like terror begins its throttled entrance because you cannot control memory. Once a memory is claimed in writing, the dominoes begin to fall. That snaking line of black and white makes an angular turn, goes back on itself, the dots careening out of control and the last memory becomes the first, knocking into the next, or the one before, and the teeming energy of life lived clatters swiftly through the tiles, and depending on how you set it up to begin with, this random display of numerical dots, each of them a memory, an event in real time, now lies exposed upon the surface of the table, itself chosen for its hoarded memories, the unbidden stories waxed into the grain. Or, if knocked in the other direction, you are faced with the blank, black, impenetrable face of denial, of eradication, of meaninglessness. So, no. When Felicity let loose her rage on the

San Francisco bus, that was not when she became an angry person. That was merely the moment she ripped off the mask of sadness and anguish and fear and pretense and longing and wanting and hoping and, yes, the bloody English politeness. *That* mask. The one she reached up for and tore from her face, exposing a near murderous rage. Because in that moment in the courtroom, when the judge had looked at her in pity and told her he was bound by the law to award custody to the New York parent because the joint custody agreement was executed there, back then, when Felicity had thought all had been reasonable, when everyone was sleeping with everyone because it was the seventies and you had the right to happiness, and if something made you happy then by extension everyone in your life would be happy, this, the hedonistic philosophy of the decade that followed on the heels of the naïve sixties philosophy that agreed with the Beatles: "Love is all you need," ta-da, da-da-dah.

Except in the courtroom there is no love. Only law and what lawyers like to call its interpretation, but which is in fact manipulation. Felicity had been manipulated by Spouse Number Two and his expensive lawyer and by the cocksucker lawyer who had been recommended to Felicity. The best, she was told. She can see him now, behind his mahogany desk, the photos of his family behind him on the bookcase, the only sign of life among the leatherbound tomes of jurisprudence and this person v. that and a thousand clauses that can form either a loophole or a noose. And she had sat there telling him her story. How she and Spouse Number Two had agreed to share custody for a year, alternating three months each with their daughter and how he had not kept to the agreement. How he had kept their child to himself that Christmas. Sending the child to her with mutual friends a week later. A year of shared custody agreed upon in order for Felicity to establish herself in San Francisco, city of beauty and possibility. The city she'd chosen instead of London, which was the city she really wanted, but at least this way both parents would be living in the same country. And they had agreed to this, amicably she had thought when sitting in Spouse Number Two's kitchen nearly a year earlier she had told him she couldn't make it on welfare and food stamps anymore. Sitting there in his kitchen. The kitchen of the house he bought himself from the sale of the house that he and Felicity had bought together, for which he had deemed her fair share of the profits to be one thousand dollars . . . minus the fifty she owed him.

Him sitting there with his new lover and her two young kids, whom he was supporting. The lover illegally collecting welfare. Felicity's predicament of no concern whatsoever.

And the lawyer who was the best had listened. Told her to go home and write an essay that night on who she was as a mother and why she deserved custody of her daughter. She gives him the essay the next day. He reads it in front of her and agrees with her. She does deserve custody. Then he says, "The problem is you can't afford me." And if she remembers correctly, Felicity had sat there nodding because it was easier to make nice than it was to reach across the desk and punch him in the face until he became unrecognizable in the eyes of the law.

Felicity blinks and looks down at the page. "Oh," she says. "Oh, this is hard." This, she realizes, is why she has never wanted to write a memoir. Because if it is to have any merit at all, she will have to be brutally honest. She will have to be willing to see every moment of cowardice she's succumbed to. She will have to see not only that the world is full of cruelty and malice aforethought, that there is no fairness, or justice for all, but that as an adult, responsibility for one's life is imperative. She will have to see that at sixteen, when she left home, she had still been a child, and while that may have been an act of courage in one way, in another it was a misguided one-way trip in search of freedom without responsibility. A search for fame without belief. A search for love without discernment.

From sixteen until forty-four, Felicity had lived with the domino effect of life lived through magical thinking, each domino a black-and-white decision made from the ephemeral mist of delusion.

But you already know all this, Felicity, what's the big deal? The big deal is putting it in writing. A recent article about Karl Ove Knausgård comes to mind. He who had let it all rip in six volumes of *My Struggle* had been publicly denounced by fourteen members of his family in an Oslo newspaper. Does Felicity want to risk losing her hard-won relationship with her daughter? Most definitely not. How about the rest of the cast of characters? Frankly, she doesn't give a shit. She may even be a tad gleeful about dissing all the assholes she's encountered in her life. But her daughter, no. She won't do that. Not after having protected her from that kind of exposure for forty-four years. Not that there hadn't been times when she had wanted to scream at her, "You know nothing. You have no idea."

On their last night together, Felicity takes her little girl to the Ice Capades. A futile attempt at distraction, of creating something magically memorable for her child. And all the while as the wee one sits mesmerized, Felicity feels herself disappearing into the ice. Feels herself cut to ribbons with every blade, the precision of metal on ice, the ice impenetrable, the blades curling and swooshing, the pretty designs so temporary, the impeding loss of her child so permanent. The cruel art of skating and she herself on ice so thin she longs to be taken beneath its surface rather than be frozen out of her child's life.

Another scene: The morning after the custody case. A small bridge in the Japanese Tea Garden in Golden Gate Park. She can see Spouse Number Two and his despicable lawyer standing on the other side, perhaps fifteen feet away. Felicity bends to hug her child. She feels the little hand patting her. "Don't worry, Mama. It'll be all right." Felicity lets her go. Watches her cross the bridge. Sees the father pick her up and walk away. There are no backward glances, but surely cruelty is in the air.

Sometime during that following week, Felicity will go to a psychic who will tell her she must wait, that her daughter will need her most when she is eighteen. Another fourteen years. Felicity feels those icy blades closing in on her. Made of mirth and steel they run circles around her, daring her to join them. But Felicity knows she must stay alive for another fourteen years, although in fact it will be much longer. Thirty-nine years later, when her daughter nearly dies, then she will finally need her mother. But back then, in the psychic's room, Felicity cannot fathom how she will survive fourteen years, anymore than six years earlier she was able to imagine surviving the death of her first daughter.

The night after the day she watches her daughter disappear from view, she will start work as the cocktail waitress at Hamburger Mary's. She will be introduced to cocaine, which, combined with cognac and the biting, sarcastic humor of the gay staff and clientele, will arm her with all the ice she needs to numb the pain.

Felicity caps her pen. How much life can be lived in a day? Soon the sun will set. She and Spouse will sit in the wicker chairs out front and watch the light turn this lamentable world into a golden globe of wonder. The hills will radiate the warmth of the day returning the light soaked into the earth. A day of truth and beauty; truth cleansing the soul; the soul reflecting its own radiance. Two strangers sitting there, woven together in the sun's last rays.

Spouse will reach for her hand. "Want to read to me?" he will ask.

Of course she wants to read to him. He is her validation. This man who has been listening to her since the evening they met. Well, all right, he doesn't always listen to her. He's a man. Let's not forget how many times she's had to scream in order to be heard. And how many women have screamed at men, "You're not listening to me!!" The historic complaint of women not feeling heard. Of saying the same thing over and over. Starting off in a civil manner; a simple request, or a statement of fact or feeling or, god forbid a combination of the two. And the good or not-so-good man nodding in agreement, the way one might give a *there there* pat to the head of a child. Then it is immediately wiped from the male hard drive. The request or statement might then be repeated with a slight edge in the tone of voice. The third repetition coming from a place of exasperation perhaps accompanied by a few tears, "But I keep telling you blah, blah, blah." And finally the enraged, "For fuck's sake are you a complete moron or do you just not have the ability to listen to anything you don't want to hear? What the fuck is wrong with you?" And then the inevitable, universal comeback in which the woman is accused of being a screaming, mentally abusive harridan. The man delivering this verdict from a place of cool, self-righteous detachment, completely oblivious as to how close he is to having his balls removed with a pair of rusty pinking shears. Because really, what the fuck, if he listened the first time around there would obviously be no need to scream in order to be heard.

But Felicity digresses. When it comes to hearing what Felicity writes, Spouse is more than attentive. He has the ability to listen on many levels at once. This is the validation that Felicity longs for, because although she is aware that there are times when her writing can edge toward sentimentality, she also knows she's capable of complex thought. In fact, what she loves most about writing, whether it's fiction or nonfiction, is discovering the way her mind has a knack of spinning out a thread, and then another, and another, ultimately weaving these disparate threads together in ways that surprise her. As if only by the act of writing can her brain fully explore the myriad possibilities that exist in the spaces between ideas.

23

SHE FIRST EXPERIENCED this quality of being heard by Spouse the night they met. She had, until then, never felt listened to by a man, with the exception of her therapist. But, not to knock the therapist without whose wisdom and intuition Felicity would never have met Spouse in the first place, still, there is an immense difference between a) paying to be heard, b) being listened to as a form of foreplay, c) being listened to by, as it turned out, a highly intelligent man who found her mind thrillingly interesting.

Nearly three decades ago they met. Cape Cod. Off season. Each of them unbeknownst to the other, drawn to watch the sun set over the ocean. Felicity on foot. Spouse on his bike. In this oft-told tale, Felicity remembers a *whoosh* as he drew level with her. He will remember the angle of the sun and how it lit up her hair like a dandelion. They will both remember the shock of that first glance and the instant letting go of it. Felicity will remember watching him literally disappear into the sunset and the almost matter-of-fact feeling of him being a kindred spirit.

Felicity doesn't remember the sun setting. What she remembers is that some one hundred yards before she arrives back at the little seaside studio she's rented, the *whoosh* returns. A long, thin figure in black spandex with silver curls beneath the rim of his helmet gets off his steed and walks beside her. They pick up a conversation that was interrupted in another lifetime. Now they are in her little studio. Names have been exchanged, arms unwinding toward each other for the handshake. The sea is a gentle slap on the sand. Felicity is lighting candles, the kettle is up for tea. They are about to sit in the gloaming and reveal themselves to each other. Felicity is twenty months sober and close to being chaste. She has no plans or desire. She is both comfortable and surprised not to be engaging in the usual flirtation. In fact, at one point she will be in a quandary. She is hot. She wants to takeoff her wool turtleneck but not only does she not want to interrupt the flow of conversation, she also doesn't want to peel off a layer of clothing and have it read sexually, even though she has a T-shirt on underneath. It is new to her, the option of communicating something as simple as "I'm hot," before removing the item of clothing. To be able to say, "I'm hot," and have it understood. To be with a man who doesn't respond to that statement with, "You sure are!" It is as though their bodies have disappeared into the night and they are merely two faces floating in the candlelight, all eyes, all ears. She isn't even aware of what she will delight in the next day; that he has succulent lips. This image Felicity has of Spouse's disembodied face in the dark, totally focused on her, is what she fell in love with. To have finally found a man who listens to her, who is interested in the all of her and not just her body. She feels a magnetic attraction that offers longevity. She doesn't understand the impact of this yet.

When he leaves, some two hours later, she feels peaceful. And she is aware that it is the first time in her adult life she has been attracted to a man and not slept with him the same day. When they do sleep together two nights later, they will hold each other only and this will be a relief. It will free her to spoon him, as she has every night that they've spent together since then. But on that night, the moon will bounce off the sea and illuminate the nape of his neck and she will look at the crosshatchings between the curls and know that this is the neck of the man she loves.

Tonight, Felicity lies in bed looking at the almost-full moon. Earlier in the evening she and Spouse had stood in the garden watching it rise above the copse of trees crowning a nearby hill, its sunlit orange face seeming to hover just above the treetops before sailing higher, the color draining to ivory as if the lack of oxygen might make it faint.

Now, bright white, it shines through the window, its beam illuminating the lower half of the duvet. Just minutes before, the light had fallen across both her and Spouse, who had turned from her, already asleep. And she had seen his neck, lit once again, the silver curls long gone, the crosshatchings deeper and of greater number and yet it is still, clearly, the neck of the man she loves. And how many fortunates experience such a thing? Decades of mapping the surface of the loved one. And, underneath the surface, the inner workings that she has come to know so well. Gone now the lusciousness of his flesh. The lips not quite so succulent, the cheeks hollowed. Where once they had licked and caressed each other they now joke about the drape of crepe they're in. But really, it isn't so funny. Not only is the joking a cover up for the absence of passion, for the pain of having closed off some essential part of themselves, it is also a cover-up for the fast approaching end . . . not of love, but of life. Those devilish moments of the reaper's visitations, which, once seventy years have been survived, will lurch upon us all. Moments of gasp and shock at the inevitability of ceasing to exist. The sorrow at times so mundane as to be riveting. Like the moment last year when Felicity had been folding Spouse's underwear and suddenly realized that one day she would not be here to ever do that again. And how, in that moment, what was habitually categorized as yet another chore became heartbreakingly vital. As though as fast as life was diminishing it was adding onto itself. How does one separate out the rage at being mortal from the rage of the unfinished, the unreconciled, the irretrievable, the mistakes and the missed opportunities, the enormous waste of time spent in opposition to, if not denial of, one's essential self?

As the moon slides past the window, the room retains a ghostly glow reducing everything in it to a hue of equal value. In that nocturnal ambience, Felicity drifts toward her angry slumber. And surely it is anger that cramps her legs, forcing her to leap out of bed sometimes six or ten times a night. What effect, she wonders, does the anger she experiences at being woken in pain, over and over again, have on her body, never mind her mental state? Does she have cramps because she's angry or does the anger come from having cramps? Shit, how much is one supposed to figure out on a daily basis? And how exhausting the continual search to figure out what she is doing wrong. For surely, whatever ails her must be of her own doing. How much of the doing is physical and how much is negative attitude? What difference does it make if you can't come up with the answer? When is one allowed to be unable to find an answer? Surely that must be the relief of death? To finally stop questioning everything? And will she go to her too-close-for-comfort death still asking what it is she had done wrong that had caused the death of her first child? Or, when the next anniversary of that baby's simultaneous birth and death comes around in a couple of months from now, will she finally understand it wasn't all about her? Will she allow that the father's herpes may have contributed to the wee soul's demise? Let's hope so. Let's hope Felicity lives long enough to tell that tale. For now, let's hush-a-bye while

Felicity comes to the surface of consciousness on this fine May day. And, if we can, let's help her save her soul.

"Give me a fucking break." Felicity leaps out of bed, calves rigid, her toes curling in different directions. She puts her hand on the window sill and leans at an angle, legs slanted behind her, forcing her feet flat to the floor, determined to ward off the cramps before they race up her thighs, which would cause her to plead for death.

"Oh god, oh god, oh god. Please, just fucking fuck off and leave me the fuck alone." There, that worked. She lets go of the sill and sits on the edge of the bed. Spouse, who still hasn't learned when to help and when to fuck off himself, has awoken and is now sitting tentatively on the edge of his side of the bed. Lucky for him that the cramps have fucked off before he had a chance to fuckup.

"Good morning," he says.

"Ya think?" she says. And another sunny day begins.

24

FELICITY SPENDS THE MORNING READING through what she has written so far and is not happy. She feels she has veered off course somewhere and is just meandering willy-nilly, following whatever memory comes to mind next. Apart from its self-centeredness, she wonders if anger and aging are a winning combination when it comes to wooing a publisher and immediately realizes that this kind of thinking is truly veering off course because, hey, Felicity, you said this one is for you and fuck everyone else.

The other thing she's not too happy with is that when it comes to aging and death, she's beginning to sound a tad pathetically like the author whose book she'd binned in town that day. Jesus Christ. When did that start happening? The creep of age? She knows when the creep of crepe started.

For a few months pre-Spouse, and early in sobriety, Felicity had been mesmerized by a twenty-eight-year-old ex-model. Felicity uncaps her pen, deciding that until she figures out what the hell she's writing about it would be quite nice to spend some time with him, literally speaking. She renames him Humphrey and giggles as she shortens it to Hump. She considers changing the last two letters to an "n" and a "k" but decides that while he for sure *had* been a hunk, the versatility of Hump being not only a noun but a verb of action would best describe their brief but intense relationship.

Felicity was about to be forty-four at the time. She was more than a year sober, as was Hump. When he'd walked into the room of a small AA meeting, his arrival had given new meaning to the "Powerlessness" referred to in the First Step. She's not sure if she'd drooled from all portals when he sat down and looked at her. She may even have looked over her shoulder expecting to see some dewy young thing standing behind her. But no. It was definitely Felicity with whom he had just slightly more than briefly locked eyes. For the rest of the hour she had struggled to pay attention to the Speaker, the Sharing, and Sobriety itself. He was just *so* gorgeous. And, as it would turn out, he would be one of the greatest gifts of her young sobriety.

Several AA quotes were affixed to the walls of the meeting room. Among the many that annoyed the shit out of Felicity was: "Expect a Miracle." She had, a month earlier, bought the bumper sticker and stuck it, tongue-in-cheek, on the rear end of her Honda Civic SI. But when at the end of the meeting Hump had asked if she'd like to get together with him that coming Saturday—and yes she did detect a slight emphasis on the word, "coming"—she was convinced that the miracle had arrived.

The gift of Hump was not only that he was a perfectly formed human being with black hair and killer blue-green eyes, the lustrous lashes of which were a cliché in that they were of the length and thickness that women spend ten percent of their lifetime income trying to achieve with mascara while lamenting that nature chooses to endow only males with such luxurious lid-fringes, much the same as it gifts the males of the avian world with exotic plumage while the female is stuck with a dowdy shade of gray, *and* has to sit on a bloody nest of eggs all day while Mr. Frigging Peacock struts, flits, and flirts with anything that moves. So there was *that*, and the rest of perfectly proportioned face with a mouth the equal of the eyes in beauty and sensuality, the truly gobsmacking bod, which at twenty-eight bore no sign of age; the muscles toned without exaggeration; the ass high and round.

Felicity pauses for a moment and lingers on the memory of that first Saturday, which in retrospect was like the pilot of a TV series in that it set the tone and pace of what would be months of physical adventure. Not just the great sex but . . . oh wait . . . it's Saturday afternoon. They go for a long hike in the country. At one point, Hump takes the lead through a narrow wooded trail. Felicity can't take her eyes of his calves. So young. So male. So damn sexy.

They go back to her house to change for dinner, lovemaking tantalizingly put on hold. And he's funny, too! Has her in stitches over whatever it is they eat. They skip dessert, knowing that something sweeter and tastier is to be had in bed.

And so it will go over the next few months. They will hike and bike through undiscovered terrain. They will fly in small planes and dance and play pool. She will get hooked on Tetris, which they play side by side in the arcade before going next door to the movies. They ice skate and sled and white-water raft and everywhere they go will be a thrill each time some woman, young or old, behind a register looks up and, seeing Hump, loses her sanity and perhaps control of her nether regions. And Felicity will feel young and ageless and beautiful and sexy and very lucky. Until one night, shortly before the end.

They are watching *Thirtysomething* . . . which neither of them are. Hump goes to the kitchen to get them ice cream. Felicity catches sight of something flashing in the periphery of her vision. She looks down and sees her forearm resting on the arm of the couch. What the fuck is that? Light from the TV screen is illuminating something stuck on her skin. She looks closer. It's her skin stuck on her skin. But surely not? There are strange lines on it. It reminds her of Christmas. Paper decorations strung across the living room. Crepe paper decorations. F-U-C-K!!!!! She has crepe skin!!

She hears Hump scooping ice cream into their bowls. She hopes the ice cream is very hard. She is playing for time. Moving her arm this way and that, checking out the other arm. She is searching for crepe-free positions. She lifts her chin because shit, maybe it's on her neck, too. She sits frozen like a human sundae waiting for Hump's return and she thinks, *really*? *This* is how I want to grow old? Twisting myself into increasingly impossible positions in order to hold on to a man who will always be fifteen years younger than me?

She leaves the house the morning he packs his stuff. She will go to his wedding the next summer. But before she's over the Hump, she will spend a couple of months riding around in her little Honda, which she has nicknamed Fonda. She will slip Linda Ronstadt into the cassette slot in the dashboard, roll up the windows, turn up the volume, and howl along with Linda, singing "Shattered," over and over. The divorce from Spouse Number Four will be finalized and Felicity will go to the spit end of Cape Cod for a week. She will come to terms with being alone. She will be sad, but grateful that she is sober, has a daughter, a house, a successful salon, and sells almost every painting she makes. She will go watch the sunset and meet Spouse Number Five. Less than three weeks later she will break her neck and never again, with the exception of making love, be able to do any of the physical things she'd shared with Hump. Her car will be totaled and towed away. The insurance company photo will show the rear bumper is the only intact part. That, and the bumper sticker, its plastic promise a prophecy come true. *She* is the miracle. She will live long enough to become a seventy-year-old author writing about anger and aging.

25

AT THE END OF THE LAST SENTENCE Felicity sits dumbfounded. Instead of writing herself out of the corner, she feels she's *become* it; two flat surfaces meeting at right angles; zero perspective. As though in revisiting the past, she has diminished the future to an infinite point of no exit. Surely she should have the protagonist turn around, facing out. But "out" then becomes a wider view of the past and she is suddenly very tired of it all.

Maybe she needs to redefine the corner, or demolish it. She could do with wielding a sledgehammer right now. Just break on through to the other side, baby. Wow. Jim Morrison. The Doors. What a name. The Doors to what? And didn't he just break on through to the other side? Felicity wonders if he found the promised land. She doubts it.

She swivels her chair away from the desk and the huge half-circular window with its view to the oak tree and the sheep pasture beyond. Now she is facing a pair of arched glass doors. She experiences a bit of dark humor at Morrison's expense. He could have used a set of doors like these. Doors to nowhere.

These open to a waist-high wrought-iron railing, which prevents one from walking out into space and the inevitable two-story drop to the ground.

Immediately she is back in time. Ten years old. A summer Saturday. She's at her school friend's house. We can call her Jill, she won't mind. Jill was one of the brainy girls in Felicity's class. Always in the top three at end of term report. But, unlike the other two who were always at the top, Jill was quiet, unassuming, almost nondescript. Felicity had wanted to be friends with her but felt she didn't have the right because when it came to grades she consistently hovered around the middle of the class. She'd had a cursory friendship with the other top two, both of them Susans. Both of them precocious, pretty, all-rounders who allowed Felicity briefly into their circle because, like them, she had been chosen to solo in the school choir. But, as seductive as their aura seemed, Felicity had suspected an undercurrent of spite; the feeling that she could be easily dismissed by them at any moment. Which, of course, would be a form of rejection. Whereas Jill, well, Jill might have seemed a bit meek, but integrity and steadfastness obviously ran deep in her.

So it was that Felicity spent a semester striving to excel in all her lessons and was rewarded at end of term when the results were read out to the class: Jill in first place. Felicity in second. She doesn't remember which of the Susans claimed third. What she remembers is lining up behind Jill to exit the classroom and asking her if she would like to come to her house for tea. So began the first kind friendship in Felicity's life. And where Jill excelled academically, Felicity excelled athletically and imaginatively and thus they encouraged each other to expand.

Oh, and Jill's parents! They were everything that Felicity's were not: generous, lenient, and you could have proper conversations with them. For three years they have sleepovers almost every Saturday night. Felicity can't wait to get to Jill's house on Saturday mornings. She felt herself to be adored and years later, on the first visit to that house in two decades, she will hear Mr. Roberts reminisce about how Felicity, or Filly, as he liked to call her, used to climb on top of Jill's wardrobe and sit there, legs swinging, eating sweeties.

Felicity encouraged Jill to do naughty things with her. Like knocking on the door of the madwoman's house and when she would open it, the girls would run down the hallway, through the kitchen, out the back door, tearing through the wild garden and clambering over the wooden fence into Jill's back garden, the old woman screaming at them.

They form their own club, which necessitates passing many tests: bounce the ball fifty times, skip rope a hundred, ten handstands against the wall. Jill's brother, three years older, scoffs at them but can be made to join in once in a while. Even brainier than his sister, Felicity has a bit of a crush on him which she covers up by teasing him.

Her favorite memory of Tony is of him playing judge at one of their fashion parades. Mr. Roberts is a carpenter and on sunny Saturday afternoons he lets them take his planks and ladders from the garage. The three kids use these as an avant-garde runway, propping one ladder against a pear tree, which leads up to one end of a plank placed horizontally between forked branches, some six feet off the ground, the other end resting in the fork of the apple tree, which in turn, delivers one to the descent of the second ladder. Attired in imaginatively draped sheets, Jill and Felicity climb one ladder, walk the plank and descend the other doing their best to offer a pirouette here and there, without breaking their necks. Tony, the judge, sits atop a stepladder rating their fashion sense and runway aplomb. Basically as kind as his sister, he inevitably declares a tie.

The Roberts family lives on the ground floor of a semidetached. An aunt lives in the upstairs apartment. Felicity finds the aunt fascinating. She doesn't understand how a relative can live upstairs and never ever be interacted with. Whose relative is she? What does she do all day? Where does she go when she goes out? As a future novelist, Felicity needs to know.

And so it is that one Saturday afternoon, when they hear the aunt leaving, Felicity persuades Jill to stand guard outside the apartment door while Felicity, finding it unlocked, enters a room which immediately appears full of information, none of which she is able to explore.

"She's coming back, hurry!" Jill's strangled whisper comes through the keyhole, followed by the sound of her footsteps tearing down the stairs. Felicity stands frozen. Hears another, heavier pair of footsteps coming up the stairs and without further thought, opens the second story window and jumps. Her fall is broken by the tarpaulin-topped coal-bin placed directly under the window. Her legs go through the tarpaulin, which rips with the force of her entry, its coarsely textured surface scraping her inner thighs, her feet, up to the ankles in coal.

Felicity returns to the present, swiveling back and forth in her chair, the glass doors to nowhere creak in the evening breeze. A bird sings two solitary notes. She thinks of the birds that sang, after they didn't, when she broke her neck. She wonders if they sang for Jim Morrison when he broke on through to the other side. She hopes the birds didn't stop singing when Tony drowned himself five years later.

26

FELICITY HASN'T WRITTEN for more than three weeks. The first houseguests of the season arrived for four days and then she and Spouse went to their favorite island for a two-week holiday.

She let herself off the hook while the friends were visiting; after all, she had invited them. And three or four days of generous hospitality felt as valid an excuse for not writing as did a snow day for not going to school. But after that, she felt it time to get back up off the curb.

She thought two weeks in a remote inn, reachable only by a small boat, would serve as the perfect writing retreat. Mornings of swimming and sunning down in the cove, a long, leisurely lunch and then, in the heat of the afternoon, a couple of hours of writing on the shaded balcony of their room, gazing up once in a while to the stillness of the eucalyptus trees, the voluptuous aquamarine sea and a hearty laugh here and there in response to the complaining bray of a donkey. Plus, there was the utter freedom from daily chores. How amazing to not even have to decide what to eat, never mind not having to do the shopping, or wash the dishes. Of course, some habits were impossible to let go of, partly because of the need to be seen as respectful and tidy; like making the bed before going down to breakfast. Even though they both knew that while they were helping themselves to a bowl of fruit and yogurt, courtesy of the goats, and slathering fresh ricotta and honey on toast, all of which were made right there from the inn's organic produce, even while they where shoving in a slice of fresh marmalade cake still warm from the oven and oh, go on, have another cappuccino, Felicity, even then the housecleaner would be remaking the bed and mopping the floor of their monastic room.

If all of that wasn't enough luxury, how about the spiritual impact of not touching money for two weeks? There was nothing to buy, unless you took the water taxi to the little port, which although enchantingly reminiscent of an Italian film from the fifties, wasn't enough to lure them away from paradise. As Felicity had pointed out to Spouse midway through their stay, the absence of commerce was soul cleansing. Indeed, it was a perfect writer's retreat. So why then on day two does Felicity come to a grinding halt? And then why does she spend two precious days in a self-blaming spiraling depression? For fuck's sake, Felicity. What is wrong with you? Get up off the curb, girl, and get back to work.

It takes her a total of three days to realize she doesn't want to get up off the curb. She wants a holiday, damn it. She has a right to that, doesn't she? Well, doesn't she? Ah, there you go. Good decision. Relax. Enjoy the bloody holiday you've been begging Spouse to take with you. A work-free, proper vacation. And so on day four, Felicity surrenders. She suns and swims and reads and eats. She finds no fault with Spouse. She judges no one. They engage in philosophical discussions with other guests, conversations of the type Felicity feels are only obtainable in Europe, where everything doesn't have to belong in one column or the other: good/bad, black/white, male/female, red/blue, up/down, rich/poor. And, joy of joys, no cell phones in evidence.

This is what they love about this place, that it attracts people with the same values as the family that owns and operates it. There is a rhythm of rightness; when you work, you do so in a focused yet unhurried way; when you vacation you let it all go. No e-mails, no texts, no postcards, and here, in this rarest of places, you are free to stare off into space for hours. And wait a minute! What do we see here? Books! Hardbound, softbound, real books. When not staring off into the unknowable horizon or enjoying intimate conversation after dinner, people are reading books. There is hope, thinks Felicity.

More than hope. There is reward. When Felicity had arrived, she had quietly placed in the library a couple of copies of her most recent self-published novel. The one she eventually wrote that takes place in that little hotel in St. Ives. You remember. Where she spent those three weeks just being. But perhaps we'll get to that later, in *this* book. For now, barely able to stop herself from exclaiming, "Fucking hell" out loud, she nudges Spouse and whispers, "Look at her." A middle-aged, bikini-clad woman from Milan lies on a lounger, itself perched on a rocky platform jutting out over the azure water below. She is reading Felicity's book!!! She will spend three days nonstop reading it . . . in English . . . at the end of which time, she will hold an in-depth conversation with Felicity on the book's merits, the emotional complexity of the characters, the clever plot, and the timely theme at its core. She will describe her utter shock at the novel's conclusion.

It will be months, autumn in fact, before Felicity realizes that during those two weeks she most resembled her name. And in that moment, sitting by the fire with Spouse, she will experience a deeper jolt of realization; that the reason why she had not been able to write during those two weeks was because she had been happy. Fuck. Fuck buggery, in fact. Because as this sudden knowledge comes down to earth like a tossed coin, the face of happiness flips over, revealing the face of anger. And Felicity will be horrified to discover that anger is the only access to creative energy she now possesses.

But that is in the future. For now, the holiday has ended and Felicity and Spouse have just walked in their gate. "Wow," Spouse exclaims, "look at this gorgeous garden you made." And indeed it is. A miracle of creative vision and hard work, it sits in the landscape as though it has done so for decades.

"Jesus Christ," Felicity says, abandoning her suitcase and bending to pluck weeds from the stone steps. "What the fuck. I'm gone for two weeks and all they do is water and mow the frigging lawn? Why can't they *weed* for chrissakes?" Spouse, in attempt to make light in the hopes of extending the holiday spirit says, "It's beneath them." Unamused, Felicity glares at him. During the next hour she will be pissed to find sour milk in the fridge, the garden hose not coiled aesthetically in its place, and by the time they unpack it will be too late to pick up the clean sheets from the laundry.

And so it is that having adequately refueled the fury tank, Felicity will be ready on the morrow to continue writing herself out of the corner.

27

FELICITY HAS BEEN SITTING at her desk for two hours. Once again her rhythm had been interrupted. This time by family. One of their kids, plus the spouse and their child, the grandchild. It was a wonderful visit, perhaps the best ever. What's interesting to Felicity is that she was on a roll before they were due to arrive and so had e-mailed them a few days earlier asking their forgiveness, but she would be needing to spend a few hours a day at her desk while they visited. They had replied so generously, and so understanding they were, and encouraging, that it had a reverse effect on Felicity. Why on earth would she want to spend time with a pissed off fictitious character when she could spend time with people she loved and who loved her?

Well, Felicity, something is shifting in you. How very sober of you. So what's the problem now? Felicity sits looking at the next blank page. She has, during these two hours, managed to distract herself several times using all known means: check for e-mail, rearrange her underwear drawer, make a cup of tea, log onto *The Times* and HuffPost in order to imbibe their toxic report on the horrendous news of the day (this particular method of distraction often ratcheting up her anger to the point where the discomfort is so unbearable that the only relief is to write).

Today, all fails to get the juices flowing. She has tried going to the divan swing in the hopes that a change of habit will kick-start her. Nothing. She tries the couch. Nothing. Argh. She espies, on the coffee table, the little black box of *Oblique Strategies* designed by Brian Eno and Peter Schmidt. A bit like a new wave version of the *I Ching*, it invites you to meditate on a current dilemma and then pick a card from the facedown deck, upon which one finds an oblique strategy for addressing the problem at hand.

Felicity holds the deck. She concentrates. Her dilemma: why the fuck can't she write today? She riffles through the cards, the way one reaches into a bag of Scrabble letters, moving them around until one "speaks" to you. She feels a card to be urgent beneath her fingers, removes it from the rest and, flipping it over, feels a shiver run through her: "Voice Nagging Suspicions." Bloody hell! How the fuck . . . ?

It's as though a bucket of cold water has been thrown at her from off-stage. Two hours of waiting for the next sentence to arrive. Two hours trying to figure out why she's empty. And the *nagging suspicion* is that she's not. She's not empty. She's full of love and happiness from two weeks of happy family. Day trips and cooking on the outdoor fire. Grandpa making a lizard trap for the curious grandchild. Lots of ice-cream cones and silly games and laughter and fly-swatting. (Felicity has been declared Nana, the Master Fly Killer by the child) and singing with wobbly voices as the car bumped over the ridges of dirt roads. Intimate talks on carefully trod ground, and hugs, so many hugs.

Felicity sits on the couch holding the card and does the math. She and Spouse have three kids and two grandchildren in New York. Felicity and Spouse go there once a year and the kids come to them once a year. If she and Spouse live to be 81 and 89 respectively, that means they'll see their family twenty more times. Twenty. The feeling that she is still a bad mother rises up in her. How could she have moved four thousand miles away? Not for a minute does she consider that two of their kids have, at various times, lived in Western states for periods of anywhere from two to ten years. Wake up, Felicity. Ask yourself this nagging suspicion: Why are you focusing on this bullshit, futile, measurement of time? Is it another way of distracting yourself from writing, or from the nagging suspicion that you are afraid to write what comes next?

A swallow, blinded by the glare of the sun, flies into the glass of the arched window. Felicity gasps, expecting to see the feathered corpse fall to the ground. Instead, she catches a glimpse of its flight. She, too, would like to flee unscathed. Why the fuck did she ever embark on this ridiculous book? Ah, yes. Anger. The corner.

She's trying to figure out when she first became an angry person. She's written enough now to know that the corner is a trap comprised of two planes meeting obliquely. Oh, she's up against the wall all right. And she wonders if the planes of anger and love will part and death take her before she let's go of the one and surrenders to the other. Because really, Felicity, for someone so desperate for love, you sure have found interesting ways of avoiding it. She caps her pen. She is not ready to write what comes next.

She calls up to Spouse, who is engrossed in his current work with a colleague. Together they are designing an online workshop in which Spouse will be the famous artist imparting his secrets.

"Want to go for a walk?" she asks.

"Can't right now," he says. "In the middle of something. How about in fifteen minutes?"

"Oh, it's OK," Felicity replies. She puts her phone in the back pocket of her jeans, grabs her sunglasses, and slips quietly out the door.

That's right Felicity, walk away; away from the desk, away from love. Walk away from it all, and when you get to the top of that pretty hill, turn around and take a good look at what you left behind.

28

FOR THE REST OF THE SUMMER, Felicity continues to write. She's grateful to have a project that allows her to stay indoors for part of the day. It's the hottest, driest summer the country has experienced in decades. In some ways, Felicity feels the climate is a metaphor for where she's at. Hot with anger, dry of spirit, not to mention vagina, but let's not go there, she thinks and has an ironic giggle, no problem, no one goes there. And like her, the land is exhausted. Fruits dry up and fall to the ground before reaching maturity. The wheat is all husk and no grain. The hills so parched that shepherds must buy food for their flocks. Olives are few, the blossoms, having come too early in the hot spring, were cruelly killed off in a freak frost. There is a feeling of danger in the arid atmosphere, the fearful knowledge that indeed we humans have destroyed the planet, robbing it of breath, suffocating it with plastic, heating it with thoughtless greed. We are literally, Felicity thinks, dying of consumption.

She wonders if her own exhaustion is a result of the heat and months of global anxiety. Or is there something lurking in her body?

It's August already, another birthday come and gone, the years like scraps of paper now, torn off, crumpled and binned. And still no sign of rain. When she looks at the land she feels thirst and doesn't know if it's empathy or early onset diabetes. And if it is? Does it matter? There are times, unbidden, when she feels now would be the perfect time to go. After all, what more of value can she produce or accomplish? She feels a prick of sadness for Spouse, who she knows will fall to his knees if she goes first. No, whoever is left standing does not win this game.

It is early evening. The temperature has cooled enough to sit in the shade of the old oak trees behind the house. Surely they groan. She thinks about the upcoming trip to New York and wonders how she'll cope with the city's relentless energy. Again, she wonders what's happened to her own energy. Has anger depleted it? Or is it a combination of her homegrown rage and that of the world?

What the hell happened? She uncaps her pen. She's been putting off writing about. . . . What Felicity . . . the state of the world? She feels her mind begin to race along with her heartbeat. A feeling of futility battles fury. Where would one start, and once started would the diatribe ever end? Every day she turns to the news, almost hoping to see that the worst has happened and every day she is rewarded because each day the next worse thing does happen. Hatred, bursting at the seams of democracy.

What are you doing, Felicity? Where are you going with this? Nowhere, she thinks. She certainly can't shed light where ignominy slithers in the slime of centuries of vile deeds. She certainly can't turn to her homeland, which long ago gave up its moral core.

And yet she can't stop, her pen furiously inking pages as she lists all that is wrong with America and England.

Finally, as if her pen is applying its own brake, she comes to an abrupt halt. Why, she wonders, does she keep returning to these political rants? After all, it's not as though she's writing anything people don't know, or that others haven't already written with more objectivity. She has the nagging suspicion it's a form of escape or defense. But from what?

She sits staring into space, waiting for some hitherto unknown truth to reveal itself. The words "America" and "England" bounce back and forth in her mind like a relentless game of ping-pong. Finally, the "ah-ha" moment drops. Of course, she realizes, these two countries, one of which she was born to and the other which adopted her, are metaphors for her two mothers. She feels about these two lands the way she feels about her mothers: abandoned by one and lied to by the other. An enormous sadness comes over her as the ground seems to go from under her. How ridiculous, she tells herself, as the tears come. Once again, she has used anger as a way of avoiding sadness, which this time comes from an even deeper sense of not belonging. It's not just that there is nothing to which she can anchor herself, there isn't even an anchor! She suddenly feels like she is the exception to the belief that no man is an island, feels herself floating blindly in space. Reality having abruptly and rudely withered like a deflated balloon.

A gust of wind sends a flurry of leaves onto the page. She looks up and is immediately taken aback by the surrounding beauty: the garden she's worked so hard to create, the olive trees, shimmering in the evening light, their ancient trunks sturdy in the ground. Such courage. And beyond the hedges and the ancient hills, the pale blue-gray triangle of a distant mountain. They will go there this weekend, to sit in its woods and grottoes, the temperature twenty degrees cooler up there, its silence full of the mysteries of the past. How, Felicity wonders, can such purity, such majesty, such unsung endurance continue to exist among the monstrosity of our prideful, soul-destroying progress? Progress? Progress toward what? Entropy, whispers one of the characters from her last novel, entropy.

Spouse, dear Spouse, comes around the corner of the house carrying his smile and a tray of drinks and cheese and crackers. As always, the sight of him lifts her heart.

"How you doing?" he asks, putting the tray down on the low wooden table.

"I'm tired," she replies. "Tired and lonely."

29

IT'S MID-AUGUST and the heat has become a cloying menace. It is impossible to remain outside for more than a few minutes, after which the heat is so oppressive it bears down on the body making it difficult to breathe. That, thinks Felicity, is the nature of oppression, like a boa constrictor it wraps around you and slowly squeezes the life out of you. And if *she* can barely breathe what the hell must it be like for all those poor souls living in oppressive regimes? The heat of this summer feels like a metaphor for all that is sickening in the world: heat devoid of a single drop of rain for months. Heat that expands itself while diminishing all else.

Of course, Felicity takes it personally. Of course, it's bloody impossible to be outside, because this is the summer that she had made a pact with herself not to do any more major work in the garden. This is the summer she would allow herself to sit and read and sunbathe in it and enjoy the thing she's made, instead of having to make it "more." How incredibly sane, she had thought, for once in her life to be satisfied with what she'd accomplished.

One lousy week she'd had before the mercury rose. Mercury, god of thievery, robbing us of illusion, of the possibility of finding solace in nature; the quicksilver rising, rising every day a little higher, and with it the distemper of the masses. Heat boiling the waters in preparation of hurricanes. Heat, sapping every stick and blade of grass to the edge of combustive wildfire.

When she and Spouse drive to town or neighboring villages, the tension in the air presses against the car. Never ones for air-conditioning, now they anxiously await its cooling effect, while out the window their beloved landscape turns brown; the earth heaving, cracking open; a thousand gaping mouths in search of quench. The atmosphere is hostile, punishing, and relentless. With each passing day, Felicity rails against it as she becomes more and more exhausted. She knows she is being ridiculous, or worse, narcissistic, but she can't stop the resentment rising in her along with the mercury. And she is sad, sad that they have poisoned the world and that it is now poisoning them. Isn't that how it works? Finally, payment comes due. But why now? Why this year, when so much else is fucked up? "I mean, really, how many more summers do we have?" she moans to Spouse, who tries to gentle her. "Think of all the ones we've had," he says.

They've just come inside after an aborted attempt at lunching under the pergola. Felicity, natch, is pissed. "What's the fucking point of being here if you can't enjoy it?" she says, slamming the tray down on the kitchen table.

"At least the house is cool," Spouse says. And so it is, the thick stone walls a protection from the heat of the sun. They long ago learned to close all windows after breakfast, in order to keep the cool of the night in and the heat of the day out.

"Does nothing ever piss you off?" Felicity asks. Spouse's propensity for seeing only the best in everything borders on idealization and she resents him for it. "For chrissakes," she goes on, "not everything is so bloody wonderful all the time. Why do you have to pretend it is?"

Oh, come, come Felicity, 'fess up. What you really resent is that you've become a "no" person and you resent how Buddhist Spouse appears in contrast to you. Sometimes Felicity wonders if she does all the inconvenient feeling for both of them, leaving him free to bask in positivity.

"I'm not pretending," Spouse protests. "I just don't see the point in getting upset about things I can't change."

"Well, fucking bully for you," she says and wonders if she's taken the default position in order to balance his unwillingness to see the fault in others. An unwillingness that has gotten them into trouble at times. She stacks the dishes in the sink, fires up the espresso machine, and begins the washing up. What she's thinking is that her becoming a "no" person is another example of the consequences of oppression, an oppression that starts with male behavior and ends with women repressing themselves in response to that behavior. And now she's really pissed. She sees how far she's allowed herself to become twisted from her original "yes" nature, instead of remaining intact, instead of continuing to be someone who could see both the yes and the no. But hadn't she too spent years in the illusion that all is good? Where is your humility, Felicity?

Oh, fuck humility. Fuck figuring it all out. To hell with the damn eternal search. Who gives a fig where she went wrong, what she did wrong, to herself, to others. Stop thinking everything is explainable, excusable, and above all, redeemable. How about this, Felicity writes, how about my hands hurt so much I could scream? How about waking up throughout the night with such ferocious pain that when the sheets touch her hands it feels like they're being flayed? How about when her hands aren't waking her, leg cramps are . . . every half hour. What happened? She used to sleep so well when they first moved here. Boasted about how she was sleeping like never before, deep and sweet and long. Waking up positive and energized. Now, after eight hours of continually interrupted sleep, she wakes at eight, both calves rigid with cramps, her feet hitting the floor, her attitude already foul.

For Felicity to perform the humble task of weeding is to be punished with pain so crippling that by evening she will neither be able to pick up or hold a water glass. That she will drop things. That she will feel effaced. Reduced. Redundant. Betrayed. Robbed. What the hell else is she *not* going to be able to achieve? Did she tell you that holding a pen is now an act of will necessitated by the indescribable need to write? Who was the asshole who suggested she use a dictation app? Does no one understand the importance of *writing* anymore? Would cave people have switched to an app had such a thing been available? Surely the manual is basic to man and woman. Surely the inscribing finger in the sand, the piece of bone or flint on the wall of a cave, the pen upon paper, the river of thought and imagination tangible upon a surface, the self plus tool engaged in crafting, deciphering thought and vision. When Felicity writes, the trail of ink upon the page is both expression and proof of her existence. It is the exquisite journey of the mind from the brain, down the neck, along the arm, to the hand that wields the pen, and yes, it *is* mightier than the sword. For Felicity, the stream of conscious thought can only be expressed manually and to feel herself gradually being robbed of this ability is to feel herself withering into oblivion. And when, she wonders, did materialism begin to rob us of not only manual dexterity but also of the connection of self to labor? When did humanity start needing more of everything? Not that covetousness did not always exist, but what a difference between today and her heyday. Now when we all must have yet another pair of shoes, another house, yacht, diamond. Big, too, they must all be big . . . apart from the shoes.

Felicity doesn't remember wanting more as a child. Well, that's a lie. She would have eaten sweeties until falling into a sugar coma. But mainly, it was "other" that she wanted, not more. She wanted different sandals in the summer, sandals that most of her school chums had. Less fussy than those her mother chose. Even then she understood that old-fashioned was a demerit. She wanted not "another" mother to add to the one she lamentably had, but an "other" one, someone else's mother. She didn't want to accrue. She wanted to trade.

She made her first trade at eleven, the year she started secondary school. The year of the fountain pen. She can see the classroom now. They are in English class. They are uncapping their new fountain pens for the first time. They begin with their names, the ink cursive on the page. The sun is slanting through the window. It's September. The window is open to birdsong. There is a hush in the room, all heads bowed beneath it. For the first time, there is no sound of a nib dipped into the porcelain inkwell. But hark! What was that? There it is again. The squeak of a nib. To Felicity this is the sound of writing; as if a pen might speak along with the writer. To Felicity *that* pen is the magic one; the only one in the room with a voice of its own. And she wants it. At the break she trades her pretty turquoise one for the nondescript squeaker. She has no idea what became of it. But in all the years since, she has hoped that another squeaky pen would find its way to her.

Finally, it does. It takes the robbery of the one with which she has written for years. The beloved pen with which she has written all those failed novels, stories, essays, plays, and poems. She is heartbroken. She orders its replacement; same brand, same broad nib. Yet when it arrives, it seems feeble. On a scrap of paper she writes with it, this way, and that. It feels miserly. She is sure it will hold her back. She's pissed off. Like a ballerina breaking in new toe shoes, she bends the nib forward over itself. She hears the kettle boiling down in the kitchen, issuing a faint whistle as it lets off steam. She makes a cup of tea and returns to her desk where she finds that the uncapped pen has rolled off and lies silently on the floor. Felicity is tempted to kick it.

Instead, she decides to accuse it in writing, "This pen is a fucking piece of shit," she writes, and as she dots the "i" and crosses the "t" she hears a squeak. "What?" she writes. "Squeak up." And it does! And it is this, this inked circle from that English classroom to her foreign desk that comforts Felicity, giving her a sense of rightness, of possibility. The possibility that if she continues to write, no matter the cost in pain, she will eventually write something of worth.

August continues its never-ending journey toward September. Along with cramps and joint pains and exhaustion, diarrhea now makes its daily appearance. She feels confused, agitated, and anxious. The most mundane chore feels like a life or death decision. She can feel the anxiety in her throat like a singed moth looking for a way out. And the anxiety pisses her off even more. For god's sake, Felicity, she rails at herself. What's your problem? Living in paradise with a good man and after all you've gone through, after all you've survived, all the bloody work you've done on yourself and you still have your finger on the sabotage button? She comes to her own defense. Who wouldn't be pissed off if they'd survived a broken neck only to waste the next twenty-seven years on writing for nothing? Who wouldn't resent continual rejection while one's spouse zooms down the corridor of yesses that are propelling him into the great auditorium of world recognition? But why, Felicity asks herself. Not why her, but why can't she let it all go? Why does she still need the very thing she deplores in others?

She's frightened now. Lately she's been wondering if all this anger and resentment are what's causing the pain and exhaustion. Is this how cancer starts? Is she eating her innards, regurgitating the bile of resentment and failure? Nightly acid reflux has now added itself to her list of complaints. The phrase "something stuck in your craw" comes to mind as she lies in the dark listening to the gentle breathing of her sleeping spouse. She feels the lump in her throat that continual belching does nothing to relieve. Thoughts of death insinuate and for a moment she longs for it, for the relief of no longer having to try harder, to figure it all out, to rise up again, try again, fail again. But she doesn't want to leave this world on a bitter cloud of pessimism.

Whatever happened to that little girl in the butterfly costume? She floats from the wings on her wings, out onto the stage, her feet a whisper above the boards. She feels the audience lean forward, feels their breath, and she soars.

30

ONE OF THE THINGS FELICITY has always loved about the act of writing is that she feels completely present and yet disappeared at the same time. Time itself disappears, along with self-consciousness. There is no sense of self when Felicity is writing. No thoughts about what she should or shouldn't be doing. Errands and chores no longer exist. Vanity? Gone. Desire? Gone. Doubt? Gone. She feels focused to the point of the nib and yet at one with the universe.

Then comes the moment when, with absolute certainty, she knows she is done for the day. She will cap her pen, and as she does, so she will feel the exhilaration that comes with achievement. Her entire body will be vibrating and she wonders if it is doing that while she is writing or if the moment she stops her being goes into shock: the way it does when waking from a dream one thought was real.

But today, although her body is vibrating, she doesn't feel exhilarated. Rather, she feels disoriented and grumpy the way one feels after napping too long. She looks up from her desk to where Spouse is usually sitting at his, but he's not there, which further adds to her disorientation. When did he leave? Where did he go?

She goes downstairs thinking to make a pot of tea. The kitchen clock shows it to be five-thirty. She'd been writing for three hours. Too late for tea. Where is Spouse? Anxiety flares in her. Did he drive into town? If so, how long ago? What if something has happened to him? She feels reality spin away from her as anxiety turns into panic.

She opens the door to the patio and calls his name. Nothing. She sees a tiny glint of metal through the hedge. The car is still there. So where is he?

Suddenly she is running round the corner of the house. Perhaps he's sunning himself on the terrace. No. Not there. She knows he would never leave her, so he must have fallen somewhere. An image of him lying somewhere, bleeding from a head wound, causes her to shout his name.

"What? What's happened?" he calls coming round the back of the house, concern all over his face.

"Where the fuck were you?" she yells at him.

He looks at her in amazement. "I was reading on the dondolo. Where did you think I was?"

"I thought you were dead," she says, knowing as she is saying it how totally ridiculous that is.

"Come here," he says, putting an arm around her and leading her back to the divan swing.

"Why didn't you answer me?" she asks, flopping down on the cushioned swing. "I was calling and calling for you."

He starts to laugh. "I thought I was the deaf one. Don't you hear that racket?" he says, jerking his head back toward the barn. And immediately, out of the silence of her terror, comes the din of the sheep, their cacophonous *baa-ing* signally the second milking of the day. Of course he hadn't heard her!

"Oh, god," she says, relief beginning to spread itself in the place where panic had so recently resided.

"How about I get us some juice," Spouse offers. "Then you can tell me how the writing is going."

As he disappears inside, Felicity tries to normalize her breathing. She starts to cry again and searches the pockets of her jeans for a tissue and gratefully finding one, gives her nose a good blow, and tells herself to shape up. Spouse returns with their favorite evening drink, a blend of ginger, apple juice, and sparkling water.

"How you doing?" he asks, as he hands her a glass and settles himself beside her. She starts to move to make room for him. "Stay," he says. "Put your feet in my lap."

Such kindness. You, she thinks, you are my anchor. Tears come again.

"What's going on, babe?"

"I don't know. I don't know what's going on. I seem to be either angry or anxious these days and it's like they feed each other. When I get anxious, I get angry with myself because really, what the hell do I have to be anxious about? So then I start to blame myself for being self-destructive and then that makes me anxious."

"Is it the writing, do you think?" he asks, and immediately she's angry.

"Why the fuck would my writing make me angry?"

"Hey, that wasn't a judgment," he says. "I was just trying to be helpful."

And now she's anxious again. "I'm sorry," she says.

The sheep have stopped complaining. Evening is beginning to diminish the day's heat, even though the air is still. Before them the garden revels in the lowering sunlight as if it, too, is relieved to be done with the day. Felicity looks at the beds and borders she's created; roses and rosemary, teucrium and lentisco and laurel, each a mere foot tall when she planted them are now shoulder high; a tapestry of texture and color, strength and beauty. She wonders if what she is writing will ever find its way to such coherence. If only this book could have such a meaningful existence.

"What's the time?" she asks.

Spouse looks at his phone. "Six," he says. "And how great we don't have to cook tonight."

"Shit," Felicity says, suddenly remembering they are supposed to go to their friends' house for dinner tonight.

"What's wrong?" he asks.

"I wish we were staying home," she says. The thought of having to get dressed, made-up, and go shine it on is exhausting. Even more exhausting is the thought of having to converse for three hours in another language when she can barely think straight in her own.

"Come on," Spouse says, his upbeat tone pricking her anger. What must it be like to always be so bloody positive, she thinks. "Really," he continues, "it'll be good to be with friends, eat good food, and have some laughs."

She knows he's right. But she also knows it will just be a temporary distraction that for a short while will convince her that the butterfly in her is still alive and well, before the curtain of despair descends again.

31

SEPTEMBER FINALLY ARRIVES, although it brings no relief from the scorching weather. It's time for Felicity and Spouse to go to New York. While they both are eager to see the kids and grand-kids, they are loath to leave their little piece of paradise, although this never-ending summer has been more like hell. What with the infernal heat, the absence of rain, and the mounting anxiety and exhaustion Felicity has been experiencing, it has been increasingly difficult to enjoy what is normally a carefree season.

As if to punish them for leaving, they are caught in a deluge of monsoon proportions on the way to the airport. Traffic on the main road crawls. The rain is being driven down from the north and Felicity fears that their plane will either be delayed or skid off the runway before takeoff. In her mind's eye, she sees a swarm of behemoths uncontrollably sliding toward one another like winged magnets.

The airport is teeming with stressed-out travelers, which, Felicity thinks, might account for how many of them are sitting in the multitude of bars and restaurants quaffing various alcoholic sedatives at eleven in the morning. Felicity can relate. These days she never flies without the comfort of knowing she has some Valium in her purse.

They make it through ticketing and security with little fuss and while away the time until departure reading, occasionally looking out the vast glass walls, so sheeted with rain that the gated planes are barely visible. Felicity's anxiety rises along with the rainfall. The blurry outline of a jumbo jet glides along a runway, the runway slick with rain. Felicity nudges Spouse. "Look," she says, pointing to the plane, "a jet stream." Spouse does not get the pun. Felicity lets it go. They board the plane on time. Felicity pops her pill and readies herself for the blissful, who-cares-if-we-crash-it's-all-meant-to-be high that will be hers in fifteen minutes.

They wait. They will wait at the gate for four and a half hours. Forbidden to leave the plane, unable to fly. Turns out that the deluge was a national event and all connecting flights have been diverted and/or delayed. Felicity is pissed. What a waste of a pill.

"What bloody irony," she mutters. Spouse, as unflappable as the plane, leans toward her.

"What, dear?"

"I said what bloody irony. Five months without rain and the day we try to leave it all comes down at once."

Thirty minutes into the delay she is already furious. Spouse will remain calm until the fourth hour and then he will start mildly whinging, but not until after he has pointed out how lucky they are to have been able to upgrade to Business. "Think what it must be like for them," he says, jerking his thumb in the direction of Economy, where hundreds of humans are wedged into their designated crevices.

By the time they arrive at their Upper West Side apartment it is nearly one in the morning. They have been awake for twenty-four hours. The kids and grandkids, who were to have greeted them with hugs and dinner, are long gone to bed. Felicity and Spouse wheel their suitcases into the spare room, shower off the filth of four thousand miles and fall into bed themselves. Up the block, a pneumatic drill begins its nocturnal feast on the street. The never-ending river of traffic whines up the West Side Highway. A helicopter whirrs above the Hudson River, no doubt carrying some hedgefunders home to their McMansions in Connecticut. It will be another fifteen minutes before the pill transports Felicity to oblivion. As she lies there in the nightglow of the apartment building across from theirs, she thinks of the first flight she ever took.

She is nineteen. She is leaving London. She is leaving England. Those were the days when air travel was still elegant. She had bought her travel outfit weeks before: a navy and emerald tartan miniskirt; a form-fitting sweater the same shade of green as that in the skirt. Her "coat" is a black PVC Mary Quant, zipped from mandarin collar to above-knee hem. She has patent leather shoes and a handbag to match. She hadn't been able to afford a new suitcase but so what, it would spend most of its time in the belly of the plane. She is excited to be leaving. She is excited to be "going" somewhere. She is young and slim and pretty and, on good days, knows it.

Those were the days when a posse of friends were allowed to come to the departure gate for a last round of hugs and cheers before going up to the roof to wave goodbye to you; that tiny little you framed in a window the size of a porthole.

She feels no fear as she goes through the gate. Why would she? She is striking out, going to a new land, one that will perhaps eradicate her roots and grow her anew. Her seat is the middle of three on the right-hand side of the plane. Two young businessmen flank her, their heads nearly touching as they lean across to assist her with the seatbelt. The adventure has begun!

Then comes the announcement that there is engine trouble.

There will be a delay while they fix it. Jesus, Felicity thinks, as she lies waiting for sleep. How come that didn't terrify me? Engine trouble? No way she'd stay on that plane today.

But the Felicity who is nineteen feels no fear. What she feels is the anticlimax, the feeling that it has all been spoiled; the feeling that whatever she embarks on somehow never turns out right. And she can feel now, all these years later, while Spouse breathes deep into sleep, the sense of abandonment, of loneliness as she, along with the other passengers, file back into the airport where they are escorted to the Sky Top Lounge for a free meal. She feels some anxiety about what might await her when she will finally land in Toronto. Will the young Canadian she'd met recently at a party still be there to pick her up? But she is young and four hours later, buckled in once again, she allows herself to feel the excitement of her maiden flight; feels so grown up, drinking little bottles of scotch and smoking cigarettes regularly proffered by her seat companions. She will stay wide awake and chatty through the night as it spools itself backward toward a Canadian evening.

It is the end of January nineteen sixty-six. Toronto is unreachable due to snow. The plane is diverted to Nova Scotia where, because it is now their first point of entry, they must go through customs and immigration. Snow-laden firs line the single runway, inscrutably dense. She is suddenly very far from home. She descends the stairs from the plane and as she steps onto the runway her little patent leather shoes slip on the ice, the ground going out from under her. One of her seatmates catches her and together they walk gingerly to the terminal.

The customs officers are two sturdy women right out of a Russian spy movie. The luggage arrives on a conveyor belt in front of them. "That's mine," Felicity exclaims, pointing to a cheap blue Woolworth's suitcase. She is ashamed to see it amongst so many luxurious ones.

"Open it," commands one of the women. Felicity takes a flimsy key from her bag, inserts it into the lock and tries to turn it. Nothing. She tries again. She feels small and stupid and is aware she's holding up the line. The "Russian" reaches under the conveyor belt, retrieves a crowbar, forces the lock and flings the lid open to reveal a hot water bottle and a flannel nightgown lying atop the rest of the contents. At first Felicity thinks it's a prank: She starts to laugh as she imagines her friends back in London sneaking the items into her case. She is sure there must be a note: *"You'll need these where you're going!"* But there is no note. Then onto the conveyor belt rolls an identical suitcase. Felicity doesn't know whether to feel relief that she isn't the only one with a crap suitcase, or mortified to have caused such an invasion of another's privacy.

As Spouse rolls over, Felicity struggles to recall the outcome of that journey, but Morpheus has the wisdom to relieve her, knowing that the journey is long and arduous and cannot be retraced in a single night . . . if ever.

32

FELICITY AND SPOUSE rouse themselves from their drugged sleep at the same moment, look at each other and share a groan and brief laugh. It's nearly noon. Thank god, they'd already decided that apart from grocery shopping, they'd spend the first day alone, free to nap and eat whenever, maybe watch a movie and get an early night's sleep. It's Saturday, and even without venturing from bed they feel the city's energy; slightly different than a weekday, a little less frantic, but still, compared to the farm it feels hyper. Felicity can feel it pressing against the walls of the building, an insistent pulse that is impossible not to get sucked into. She's been awake three minutes and is already anxious about all there is to do: unpack the suitcases, check the kitchen and bathroom for supplies—it's been nine months since they were here. She'd better get fresh towels out, write the grocery list. Shit, what about breakfast? They'd arrived too late to shop for food.

She flings the covers back, her feet groping for her slippers. Damn. She forgot to pack them.

"Take it easy," Spouse says.

"Take it easy?" she asks incredulously and begins to rattle off the list of things to be done.

"It's OK," Spouse says. "I'll go get some breakfast things while you take a shower."

She sits back down on the edge of the bed, anxious, exhausted, disoriented. Spouse strokes her back and she feels sorrow rise in her like a captive dove. She wants to be held without either of them stirring. A silent embrace to sink in to, surrender to, without desire or fear or resentment. Can a woman actually be held without offering anything in return? Either out of her own ingrained sense of obligation, or the certain knowledge that something more will always be expected of her?

It will be another month before women begin unleashing their accusations of sexual harassment. Yet even though she cannot know this, she feels the rising tide of women's wrath from centuries of having their bodies plundered, every orifice violated. And lest the tongue might wag it will be severed.

"Come here," Spouse says, pulling her gently back into his arms and her sorrow becomes barbed, her need, her vulnerability, her longing for solace, cauterized by the searing flame of anger. Why is he always too late? She pulls away, leaps from the bed. It's afternoon for god's sake. Get the bloody breakfast already. Like ticker tape the to-do list begins its scroll again: suitcases, laundry, shopping, the kids, the grandkids, and all the friends who expect them to divide themselves into twenty pieces in three weeks. She looks back at Spouse and sees the river through the window. A barge slides between two buildings like a slug between stones. She turns away and sees a Tuscan landscape on the wall, a large Joel Meyerowitz photograph they'd splurged on a few years earlier after an unexpected flurry of sales of Spouse's work. She looks at the rolling hills, the vast sky, the absence of electric lines. The atmosphere pulses off the laminated surface and she wishes she were there and not here. Immediately, as always, when she has the urge to fulfill her own need, she feels the guilt of abandoning the children, especially her daughter. Oh, for heaven's sake, Felicity! The "kids" are in their forties, and they live where they choose to live without giving a thought to you. "Stop it," she mutters. She will not bring the children into this. The decision was made months ago. They will exist in privacy, off the page, unless she has something wonderful to say about them. In the abstract, of course. No details. No particular events, no. . . . And now she is angry that after all those years of not giving a damn, now she wants to be the good mother. Now she will protect them, even at the cost of her own life. For this is her life she's writing about. How do you excise a child from the sum total of a life? How do you say, I made mistakes, she made me pay, she had the right, it nearly killed me, and leave it at that, when it's never just that, when redemption has been allowed, when a child nearly dies and the disease that the child must live with becomes the cure for the malady of estrangement? No, enough. She really must try not to go there.

Instead she goes into the shower. She feels dizzy. Sits on the edge of the tub for a while. Must have stood up too fast. Hungry too. Druggy sleep. Anger, anxiety, longing, fear, resentment, joint pain, cramps, diarrhea, confusion, exhaustion. Come on, Felicity, pull yourself together. She stands under the shower, looks down at her body. She still has good form. Knows she looks great in clothes, especially from behind. But the naked crepe situation is horrifying. How come you don't know about this when you're young and firm and insecure? She has a sudden flash of pure ivory skin on red silk. A few years back. A young woman, smoothing the fabric that Felicity will have made into curtains. She had watched the hand in jealous amazement: the pale, flawless, vein-free hand, caressing the blood-red silk. She had wanted to say to the girl, "Stop! Look, now. See your youth. Admire your beauty. Cherish its fleeting moment."

She must have been in the shower longer than she realized because by the time she's toned, serum-ed, creamed, made-up, and gelled, Spouse has been out to the store and is now scrambling eggs. Bread is toasting; the Nespresso machine is fired up, table set, and a dozen red roses vased upon it. Unaware of her, Felicity watches him as he sets the napkins straight, head tilted to the side in appraisal.

"I'm so sorry," she says. He looks up.

"What for?"

"For everything."

The eggs cool on their plates, the toast remains unbuttered, and the Nespresso machine blinks itself off as Felicity lets Spouse guide her to the couch. September light, reflecting off the Hudson River illuminates the apartment. A sailboat drifts downriver aided by the outgoing tide and a northern breeze. Felicity, awash in tears, herself adrift, wonders if death will feel like that, a sudden turning of the tide sweeping her out to the last horizon. Spouse, for once remembering not to go into rescue mode, merely sits next to Felicity and lets her cry until she keels over, head in his lap, sobbing like a frazzled infant.

"I don't know where I went," she says.

"What do you mean?"

"I mean I don't feel like me anymore. I feel old and bitter and resigned and I'm frightened."

Spouse starts to say something. "No," she says. "If I don't know, how can you possibly know?"

She's too tired to pull away. "I seem to have become someone I'm ashamed of," she whispers. He strokes her head and she remembers him telling her that when he first saw her he had wanted to get off his bike and stroke her head. And she remembers how, shortly before she met him, when she thought of being with a man again, she had envisioned not some hunk who'd fuck her up against a wall, but a man who would stroke her head after a hard day. And now, here she is, after a hard year, and her man is stroking her head and she wants to let go and feel only that. But what she feels is annoyance that he's doing it against the direction in which her hair grows so that she feels ruffled instead of soothed. And isn't it just that easy for humans to disappoint each other? Why can't she just grow up and gently ask him to stroke her the way it feels good to her? When did she start turning disappointment into irredeemable judgment?

She doesn't remember falling asleep. When she comes to, the light is failing. The last flash of setting sun is lighting up the bookcase. The spines of novels, poems, essays, myths, and memoirs, luminescent in their achievement. Books she has read and reread. Books she has studied for her master's degree. Books she has lived in, laughed at, cried over. Books that inspired, amazed, angered. Books that imparted wisdom, absurdity, audacity. Shelves full of soul and heartache, invention, and courage. Grief, too. And in the middle of all those authors, her journals. More than seventy of them. Forty-five years worth of dreams and rantings, yearnings, ideas, drawings, poems, heartbreak, irony, perseverance, belief. Lists of lovers, resolutions, and possibilities. In the cupboards under the bookshelves lie her critical and creative theses, her manuscripts of stories, novels, poems, plays, essays, folders of rejection letters, letters of interest, but not this time. Not this one. Thanks, but no thanks. There, where the sun don't shine is the asshole of her achievement.

She hears Spouse in the kitchen. Something smells good. He feels very far away. Slowly, she pads over to him.

"Good evening," he says, turning to her with that still-boyish smile. "Hungry?"

She feels so weak. "Must be," she says and sits on the floor.

"What *are* you doing?" he asks. He leaves the stove and looks down at her.

"I think I'm dying," she says.

She feels the words whisper past her lips. A death sentence. Will she gasp at the end? A faint smile hovers and is gone. She thinks about getting to her feet. It would be the sensible thing to do. She feels no pain. Just an absence of physical ability. She remembers trying to get out of the car when she broke her neck, but apart from her eyes and mouth, no part of her body responded to the brain's instruction. Then there was pain. Awful, searing, screeching pain. In her chest and up her arms. And she couldn't understand how you could feel so much pain and yet be paralyzed. Surely paralysis was numb?

Once again, her body will not respond to her brain's command. But is it a command or a half-hearted hope? Instead of rising to her feet, she surrenders to the floor, lying there as if it were the natural thing to do. She doesn't feel faint. She knows what faint feels like. No, this is just a slow shutting down, a fading away. Spouse is on his knees now and she sees the disbelief, the agony of his impending loss carved into his face. She would reach for him if she could. Instead, she whispers to him. She is totally at peace. Warm. Soft. Filled with love and acceptance. "It's all right," she says. "I've had a good life." She is holding him with her eyes.

"Don't worry," she says. "You'll be all right." He's reaching for his cell phone with one hand and holding her hand with his other.

"Don't go," he begs, "please don't go." She feels her hand in his: a mourning dove fallen from its nest.

"It's all right," she whispers. "It's all, all right. All of it. What we've had. It was everything."

The calm she feels now is the calm after the storm of her life. The calm of letting go. She is transported back in time to her car, its front end concertina-ed, the silent world before the birds began to sing again. The mighty decision to live, at any cost. The flame of her like rocket fuel lit for takeoff. The kernel of understanding unfurling like a chrysanthemum bud in hot water. Your life, Felicity, this is your life, not your death. The knowledge, then, that she could overcome her mother's warning, could enter another realm of being that held possibilities of which the old one had been ignorant. The spirit of her whole, like it hadn't been since her mother walked away from her after birth. The knowledge that mothers were no more to be trusted than any other. The myth of belonging shattered in infancy, in newborn-ness. Innocence already a thing of the past, dead in the umbilical cord. Her spirit split then: half indomitable, half in shock. A tiny mortal in a hospital crib, rent in half. Then, forty-four years later, less than a hair's width from death, her whole spirit had risen up in harmony with acceptance of life.

Now, here she is in acceptance of death. Not even surprised. Relieved even, here at last is the ultimate snow day, authoritative permission to do nothing, go nowhere. Except she is going, quietly.

Back then, in her totaled car, she went nowhere. Not for an instant. Conscious through it all. Aware of the necessity for vigilance, for self-responsibility. Only on the morning of the surgery, her head and neck already immobilized by steel rods, had she experienced doubt. Two friends stand by her bed while the anesthesiologist explains the pre-op process, telling her that he knows she's in recovery and her laughing, saying, "Oh, you mean the surgery is over?" Knowing full well that he's referring to her Twelve Step recovery, but never one to miss the chance for a laugh. And then the sudden knowledge that the death she had escaped on the road might be waiting for her at the tip of the scalpel. She starts to weep. Tells her friends to write down her will. The house she'd purchased with a down payment courtesy of the meager settlement from the meager spirit of Spouse Number Four. The house, the piano, upright, black, and sonorous. Her paintings, journals. The few photos not burned by the paranoid lover who beat the shit out of her, all of it to her daughter. And her shoes, of course, the most coveted of all by her then teenage daughter. And with a one, two, three, she's on the gurney, in the elevator, the enormity of knowing this might be her last ride, a descent, of course. Her friends' stricken faces as the doors slide closed.

Spouse has left the door to the apartment open for the paramedics. He is leaning over her begging her to come back. Later he will say he saw the life go out of her. And who will ever know why she changed her mind? Did she even have a mind in that place to which she briefly journeyed?

The paramedics are asking questions, which Spouse answers. Felicity hears jet lag, hunger, stress, not herself. Once again, she's lifted onto a stretcher. Once again, the descent in an elevator. Wheeling across the lobby she sees the worried face of the evening doorman. She's still in her nightie, and for a moment wonders why she didn't get dressed after her shower. It's a September evening. Saturday. The air is cold. In the ambulance, an oxygen mask is administered and she wonders if that means she doesn't have to breathe anymore. And she wonders why Spouse called for an ambulance. He knows that she doesn't want to die in a hospital. They are heading north. Why is there no siren? Not dying, perhaps? And then she's back in that other ambulance, paralyzed from the neck down and the siren parting traffic.

It's Felicity's fourth ambulance ride. The first, when she was eleven, she barely remembers. She had been sent to stay with acquaintances of her parents. Younger than them by a couple of decades, this couple had a one-year-old boy who had adored Felicity from his highchair, his pram, and his crib. She had no idea why she'd been sent to these people and even now, sixty years later, can only speculate upon the secrecy of her parents' lives. A secrecy in which she was enshrouded from the moment they adopted her.

What she remembers about that week is the love, the joy, the kindness she felt in that house; the way she was treated as someone of value. Even the dog would leave his rubber bone in her suitcase before she was whisked off to hospital.

It is the day before her parents are to collect her. She awakes with a severe headache and is unable to move her neck. Meningitis is doing the rounds and even now she can see the mother, Sybil, her name was. She comes into Felicity's bedroom to wake her and when Felicity describes her symptoms, she sees the mother retreat. Suddenly, Felicity is a danger. The mother must protect her own child and it is shockingly clear to Felicity whose child *she* is. For hadn't she fantasized that she would stay with this family forever? Hadn't she wished, without shame, that her parents were, if not dead, at least departed?

Was Felicity afraid then? She thinks not. She would already have been fastening her hope onto the hospital. Anywhere but home. She was in the hospital perhaps ten days. She liked it. Liked the starched blue-and-white uniforms of the nurses; the cribs and beds of the children's ward, crisply made each morning; and in the night, the tick of the huge, tiled furnace in the center of the ward.

Her parents don't visit. Her brother does. Eight years older and the hero of her childhood, he too had escaped home at sixteen . . . if joining the army can be called an escape. She remembers the day he left as if he were a lover leaving; bending over her bed in the predawn, kissing her goodbye while her little heart breaks.

Three years later, he comes to visit her in the hospital, journeying on his Lambretta from the barracks where he is stationed, some fifty miles away. Allowed to see her, even though it is after visiting hours. He is a British soldier and therefore has a right. He brings her jellied fruit pastilles. They lie in their box like jewels. When he leaves, she is bereft and when the nurse confiscates his present she is horrified to discover that cruelty is hidden in the folds of the starched uniform.

She didn't have meningitis. Who knows what it was. In retrospect, Felicity feels sure it was a first attempt at escaping her parents.

Back in New York, the ambulance pulls up to the hospital bay. She is unloaded and wheeled to the emergency ward where she will lie in a corridor listening to the wails and groans of the wounded. It's Saturday night in Harlem. Guns and knives and insanity are involved. Blood is taken, an IV hooked up, questions asked. Another gurney arrives. Felicity hears the woman on it muttering, lamenting. Her anguish permeates Felicity, who turns on her own gurney to reach for this soul. And soul is nearly all that's left of this old woman. Her steel-wool hair a shade of gray close to the pallor of her skin, which once must have shone like dark satin. Now she is becoming a shade, leaving this world in distraught solitude. Felicity reaches for her, "I know," she says. And the bony hand reaches for hers as she is wheeled away. A flicker of spirit enters Felicity. She turns to Spouse. "It's not my turn," she says.

It's nearly midnight. Felicity and Spouse hold hands in quiet desolation. All around them doctors, patients, and the not-so-patient are busying themselves between the layers of life and death. Where earlier, devastation had etched itself deep into Spouse's face, exhaustion now resides, and maybe a hint of resignation. On this evening, they understand the nearness of death. They understand they are lucky to have escaped it for so many decades, but it looms now, the horizon so much nearer; the knowledge that barring a catastrophe, one of them will be the last one standing.

Felicity closes her eyes and listens. The squeaking wheel of a gurney, the groan of the wounded, the metallic clatter of a curtain drawn along its rail. Machines beep and whistle and hum; blood pressure cuffs puff like old men; a needle clatters into a tray; a stream of piss splashes into a bedpan. Nurses and doctors instruct and confer in varying degrees of compassion and indifference and over and around them all wafts the faintly metallic smell of blood mingled with disinfectant. The blanket Felicity had asked for an hour before finally arrives and Spouse gently tucks it around her, kisses her forehead. "Thank god, it's not your turn," he says.

Birth. Death. Felicity used to think they were the brackets between which life was lived. Now she feels that death is the constant with which one resides. The ultimate reality. She hopes it will be hilarious. As for birth, Felicity feels that after the initial entrance onto the global stage, it is merely a metaphor with which we deceive ourselves into believing it can be repeated at will; that we can be born again: Christians, recovering addicts, transgender, vegan, Buddhist. Born again into some new enhanced self. As she lies there semiconscious, Felicity sees the journey of life not as a series of possible rebirths but more as an optical illusion in which we change shape: physically, emotionally, philosophically. Twisting ourselves this way and that in order to avoid pain and responsibility and disappointment. There is only one birth for each of us, and in that moment, that slim, fleeting moment, we are our essential selves composed of DNA, placental nutrition, and the mystery of our individual spirit, all of which will be continually tested, repressed or encouraged, thwarted or fertilized, pressed upon by the countless rules and regulations of our circumstances, nationality, race, gender, ability, disability. Talents will emerge and blossom or remain latent. Desire will be fulfilled or unrequited. Success will be granted or denied or, if wisdom prevails, will be redefined. History will be imparted lie by lie. Religion will be warped according to the need of the discriminator. And all of this will wash over the newborn as the cord is cut and the body weighed. If we are fortunate we will go from inside the belly to on top of it, experiencing both belonging and separation; the first duality of being. Or we will be renounced to the arms of a nurse or an incubator, to a doorstep, dumpster, or orphanage. However we shall run the course of our lives, from that moment the destination remains the same. We are headed in one direction only, no matter how many detours we take, no matter how many pills we swallow, no matter how many push-ups we perform, no matter the Botox, the lipo, the lifts, the juice bars, and the gyms, the islands in the sun, the size of your cock, the wetness of your vagina. No matter the youth, the beauty, the hare-lip, the title, the slum, the food stamps, the off-shore accounts . . . death is a-coming.

Felicity thinks of the times she's nearly died, or wished to do so. They appear now, the way it is said one's life scrolls before us on our deathbed. Now here she lies, possibly to live another day and it is her near-deaths that visit.

She was told that whooping cough nearly claimed her at four, but she has no sense of that. She remembers the cough, painless and animal-sounding. She can hear her parents conferring with the doctor who thinks she should be hospitalized and Felicity will never know if it was her mother's intuition that kept her home or her unconscious desire to be relieved of this child that bore no resemblance to her. She no longer blames her mother; in fact, she feels compassion and sorrow for her in that she was not equal to, nor understanding of this orphan child whose energy and cheek were already being shamed. So let the poor soul go and be grateful it wasn't worse. And yet what pain, what loneliness, what constant fear of punishment caused fifteen-year-old Felicity to attempt her first suicide? The howling absence of kindness. Simply that. The constant disparagement and criticism, the fast slap across the face for some careless dropping of a plate, her face slapped red before the china shattered on the tiled floor of the kitchen.

A young doctor arrives. He informs Felicity and Spouse that she is suffering from severe dehydration and exhaustion and recommends a complete physical with her general practitioner as soon as possible. And that's that. The I.V. is removed. A wheelchair arrives. Spouse helps her into it, tucking the blanket around her. "Oh, no," she says. "We have to leave that here." She already feels guilty to have wasted everyone's time, not to mention scaring the shit out of her husband.

"Fuck it," he says. "It's the least you deserve."

Autumn is in the air; the only sign of nature on this forlorn street. They are at the curb, hoping for a taxi. They get away with the blanket, but not the wheelchair. Felicity stands barefoot in the filth of the city, Spouse's arm around her. He gives his Bronx whistle and a yellow cab pulls up. There is no greeting or offer of help. In the back seat Felicity lolls against Spouse. "I am so sorry," she says.

"No problem, babe. Most fun I've had in a long time."

The dinner Spouse had been preparing when Felicity collapsed still sits half-cooked in the wok. It's nearly one-thirty in the morning and neither of them are in the mood for a chicken veggie stir-fry.

"You have to eat something," he says.

"Toast with almond butter and honey?" Felicity suggests. "And chamomile tea."

"Get into bed," he says. "I'll bring it in."

"You're the best," she says and shuffles off to the bathroom. She sits on the edge of the tub to wash her feet, watches the gray soapy water gradually run clear. Would that it were that simple, she thinks, to rid herself of whatever ails her. She puts her nightie in the hamper and takes the spare one from the hall closet allowing herself a kudo for keeping a few items of clothing in New York. On the same shelf she sees a couple of pairs of socks and could weep with gratitude to find them there. Her feet are so cold. Propped against the pillows she sits in bed and gazes at the river, a dark, silent snake undulating between the buildings. It's not the bed she wants to be in nor the view she wants to live with, but she is alive to see it.

She hears the toast pop up in the kitchen. The kettle will whistle soon and she lets herself drift back in time to a lowly flat in Chelsea. She is seventeen and wildly in love with a twenty-eight-year-old Australian. We'll call him Bernie. What the hell, he's probably dead or deaf or diseased by now. But then . . . oh . . . then he was an irresistible rascal. Curly brown hair, the hazel eyes, unwavering as they look at her. That mouth, the corners curling into a devilish smile that earns him forgiveness every time he strays. A man-boy, lacking all responsibility and discipline except when making love and that he does with languor and lust, balanced for as long as she needs him to be on the fine line between pleasure and orgasm. He teaches her how to fry eggs and this she does on the mornings that he has stayed over. Rising at five-thirty to put on her make-up and then creeping back into bed in order to fake waking up with him when his alarm goes off at six. And every morning she hopes he will forgo the eggs and have her instead. But this is a man who feeds his appetites as they arise. And so while he showers, she fries the eggs.

He breaks her heart a hundred times. And on the Saturday nights when he stands her up, she wails along with the Righteous Brothers, *"You've lost that loving feeling."* Then, when she can wait no longer, she crawls into bed, leaving the French door ajar just in case. And there are times when she drifts between sleep and waiting that the air will shift and suddenly there he is, standing in the doorway, the night on him, his helpless smile immediately melting her.

She had been too old, too wise, to have her heart broken by Spouse. Not that he hadn't bruised it in the early years. Not that she hadn't considered the possibility of letting him go. But they had both signed on forever, back then when forever seemed a possibility. They were still here, weren't they? Spouse, her Spouse, really the only true spouse of them all, was coming down the hall carrying tea and toast to her. A helicopter whirrs over the river. She turns to the window and sees Spouse superimposed over the nocturnal pulse of the city.

Spouse is the first of Felicity's husbands whose name she has not taken. She marvels that it took her so long to not only find Mr. Right, but to realize that nobody belongs to anybody, in spite of centuries of men thinking otherwise. When she had divorced

Number Four, she had taken back the name of her blood mother, which, ironically, was Best. And while Felicity could claim neither of her mothers as being the best, when she chose to become Felicity, in pursuit of her right to happiness, she had also decided to aim for being the best she could possibly be and so had taken that surname as her own. When Spouse had finally proposed to her she had told him that she would not be taking his name but that he might consider taking hers seeing as he was the best of them all.

And here he is, complete with bed tray which he places over her before returning to the kitchen to fetch his own, which Felicity holds for him while he settles himself next to her under the covers.

"I thought I'd lost you," he says, and a tear runs its course. Felicity wipes it away before it drips down his neck. "It was unbearable."

"I'm sorry," she says. "Not just for tonight but because in a way I've been lost to both of us for a while, haven't I?" He starts to say something. "Ssshh," she says. "It's late. We're exhausted. Let's eat and sleep and take a fresh look at it all tomorrow."

He turns to her. "I've missed you," he says, and takes a bite of his toast.

Is it because she's exhausted, or that maybe she is ill, or that once again she won the toss against death, or is it all of it that makes her feel like something is shifting in her? They drink their tea in silence. Felicity thinks of the woman on the gurney. Sees their hands reaching for each other, two strangers in search of comfort. And isn't the world so cruel that it wouldn't let them touch? The attendant, not attendant at all. Could he not see? Could he not have stopped for just one second? What's the use of measuring time if it can't include an inch of kindness? One touch before death takes all.

Spouse takes the trays back to the kitchen. She hears him cleaning up. She remembers sitting paralyzed in her crushed car. The other driver is getting out of his vehicle and comes to the window on her side. She cannot turn to him. It's October. The window is rolled up so perhaps he cannot hear her ask him to hold her hand.

She sees him in her peripheral vision, standing there like a pale shadow and then he's gone and she never sees or hears from him again. Ever. A man nearly kills her and is incapable of saying sorry.

Later Felicity will joke about how there are two things a man cannot do: one is to say he's sorry and the other is to ask for directions. But it's not so funny really. To be unable or unwilling to admit that each of us causes, to some degree or other, harm and disappointment to others and not be able to make amends for so doing is to be lacking in compassion and humility. To be unable to ask for help, to admit to not knowing how to get somewhere or achieve something is a hubris that scores us with loneliness.

Spouse joins her under the covers and switches off his bedside lamp. She turns to him, spooning him one more time. It's a moonless night but she knows the map of his neck and in her mind's eye she sees every line the years have etched into him; all the roads and crossroads and byways that it has taken him to get here, right now. She reaches for him, strokes his neck. "You really are the best," she whispers.

They wake earlier than they'd thought they would, given the hour they'd fallen asleep. They turn on their phones, each of which utters a series of beeps and alerts, messages from the kids: *Where are you? Call me. Are you OK? Getting worried now.* Surely it wasn't that long ago when these were the types of messages they had left on the answering machines of their young adult children. They decide lying is appropriate just this once. No need to worry them. Turned out to be nothing anyway, nothing some sleep and hydration couldn't fix. They'll tell the kids the partial truth; they were exhausted, fell asleep early, let's all have dinner together tonight, can't wait to see you.

And Felicity *is* exhausted. Her hands hurt, she has a cramp in her right leg, but she's too tired to be pissed off. By the time she's showered and had breakfast, all she wants to do is lie on the couch. "I tell you," she says, "This getting older stuff really sucks. Used to be I'd hop on a plane and go anywhere, anytime and be ready to rock 'n' roll on arrival."

"I'm not exactly high energy myself," Spouse says. "Traveling definitely takes its toll."

"Yes but . . ." she starts to protest.

"But nothing!" Spouse interrupts. "It's not just jet lag this time. Look what we went through last night. Speaking of which, you're to call the doc tomorrow morning. In fact, we should both get check-ups while we're here."

After breakfast, Felicity curls up on the couch with her manuscript and pen. She's not sure if she has the energy to write, but it's a good moment to read what she has written so far and see how it holds up, what it's lacking, where it needs to go. All of which, she muses, are questions she could apply to herself. She checks the time on her phone and sees she has nearly eight hours before the kids and grandkids arrive. She's dreading seeing them, which confuses her. After all, they are the reason for this trip.

It reminds her of when she had her salon and the times she dreaded seeing the next client. Not because she didn't like them. In fact, she loved her clients. Had learned after the first year that she had a right to choose who she took on. Amazing that during those seven years before she broke her neck, nearly six of them had been before she got sober. Yet as wrongheaded as most of her thinking had been during her alcoholic career, there were moments of clarity, of wisdom, of self-worth even.

A memory of the alcoholic and—as Felicity later found out—crack-addicted mother whose baby she had delivered comes to her. Once again, she sees the poor woman hugging goodbye to her little girls before they get on the school bus. How complex we are, Felicity thinks. That a mother can wash and clothe and send her kids off to school on time while a third lies in her womb ingesting a percentage of that same mother's daily dose of crack cocaine?

The last few years before Felicity sobered up were a bit like that. Some part of her that the alcohol and cocaine had not yet diseased functioned at a high-enough level to fool her clients and some of her friends and certainly herself, although not her daughter she would later discover.

Felicity's salon was her temple. The place she went to five mornings a week, most of them with a hangover. But every morning when she saw her name on the front of the building, every morning when she inserted the key into the door, she felt pride in her achievement. So she was an alcoholic and drug addict, still she'd come a long way since food stamps and welfare. So her fourth marriage was unraveling; this salon was hers, designed by her, furnished by her, with her art on the walls, and she was good. Damn good. And she knew it. Within nine months of opening the salon there was a three-month waiting list for an appointment. And this she had achieved perhaps because she was still young enough at thirty-seven to override her addictions in this particular compartment of her life. The drive to be independent, to achieve success, had somehow grown not, as she mistakenly thought, because of cognac and cocaine, but in spite of them. She had perfected the fuck-you that was born on that San Francisco bus. Sure, she'd gone all the way down first. Well, you had to if you wanted to finesse the fuck-you. You had to live in cabins without electricity and running water, start your car with a paring knife inserted into the ignition. You had to become a poet reading bitter lines that searched for beauty, even then; you had to drink with the bums in the parking lot, jerk off the coke dealer in order to extract a couple of lines from the pouch he kept under his greasy leather cap. You had to forgive men who beat you up, who threatened to kill you if you told. You had to sleep with a knife under your pillow and stand in a parking lot on Saturday morning watching Spouse Number Two drive off with your child just as the church bells finished striking the appointed hour. You had to fuck and hope for the best, and when the worst happened, you sold your first two wedding rings to pay for the abortion, and when you crept, still bleeding into the bed in the spare room of an alcoholic couple's house, you had to plead with the husband not to fuck you. You had to take your kid to Happy Hour on the weekends you were allowed to have her, so that she could eat the free nuts and cheese and crackers at the bar while you nursed a drink. You had to hope like hell you wouldn't be called in to cover someone else's shift on those weekends because who would look after your child? You had to sleep with any man who had a glint of magic just to keep believing; the has-been musicians, the out-of-date hippies, the lonely dentist, the carpenter who brought you flowers then beat the crap out of you and burned all your photographs. You had to keep on saying "fuck you" until the rescue came. And when the rescue that was Spouse Number Four turned out to carry envy and betrayal you had to bear with it until you got your license to cut hair, to create the Best Salon and give the best haircuts. No longer needing to give head, now you could hold them as you shampooed them, cradling the lonely and the unloved, the vain and the timid, the competent and the yearning. Holding heads that hadn't been held since infancy. Holding them. Massaging them. Watching a tear slide into an ear. Swaddling them and leading them center stage to be cut and styled. To be respected and adored for thirty minutes. To see themselves through your eyes. To be made beautiful in their uniqueness, to be listened to as they doubted and mourned and hoped and believed. This, Felicity did fifteen times a day, five days a week for seven years. Through hangovers, snowstorms, a failing marriage, and mothering the teenage child who had temporarily chosen her over the father. Seven years of being thanked fifteen times a day, five days a week; thanked for helping people look the best they could ever have hoped for. Then she broke her neck and it wasn't only her car that came to a screeching, smoking halt. It was her whole life. The life she had been soberly building ended the moment metal hit metal at fifty-five miles an hour.

And yet, on those days when someone canceled at the last minute, Felicity would dread having to deal with the following client as if the break in the rhythm gave her time to doubt herself. But no, that wasn't it. If there was one thing she had ever known for sure it was that she was a great haircutter. Maybe it was more a feeling of suddenly not knowing who she was or what her true purpose was.

It was a little like being a new mother. When the baby was at breast looking up with adoration, there was nowhere else Felicity had wanted to be. But when the feeding and burping were complete and the baby once again asleep, Felicity would feel lost. Would have no idea what to do with herself. There didn't seem to be enough time between feedings to step back into that other life, the life she had before becoming responsible for another human being. It was almost as if she dare not to do anything for herself before the child woke again, because to be interrupted by the crying infant was too extreme, too jarring. Then she might not know how to become a mother again. And so she would sit, partially paralyzed, waiting for the call to duty, and dread would befall her. The dread that so many new mothers feel but must never admit to. And it was crazy-making, this twilight zone, where you were neither one thing nor another. Where somehow you were suddenly never enough for yourself or for your child. And the irony of feeling utter love when actually in the act of mothering and yet dreading the next opportunity to feel that love has always confused Felicity. It was as though she were two separate people. So that the things and the people she loved the most, she also resented. Those gaps between breast-feeding and later between clients, seemed to echo with the emptiness at her core. The feeling that there was something else she was supposed to be doing with her life. And fear. Terrible fear that she wouldn't be able to sustain either the creating or the loving. That maybe, like *her* mothers, she had a limited ability to love. Or was that just the mirror reflection of a bottomless need for love?

And here she is, still, all these years later, torn between the desire to write and the desire to see her children and filled with fear that she will do neither well enough. What a load of self-indulgent bollocks-y shit, Felicity.

33

THIS IS NOT GOING WELL at all. Have you stepped out of character, Felicity? Have you given this job to someone even less well equipped than you? What's with the nearly dying and then going all passive and tiresomely introspective? You want to write in psychobabble clichés, then where is the fire in your belly? I mean one minute you're raging on a farm in some unnamed land, with an unnamed spouse, and the next you're in New York having a convenient collapse. Oh. No. I don't think so. You don't get off that easily. In fact, there seem to be a few missing months between chucking the book on literary death, which, correct us if we're wrong, but wasn't that in the late spring? And then it's steaming August. And the next thing you know we're touching down at JFK and riding the Saturday night ambulance to a Harlem hospital. I mean, OK. We get it. You've been ill for a while. Longer than you realized, and sure, maybe this will eventually explain a lot, but then what? Sounds like an early wrap, no?

Where did all the anger and resentment and bitterness go? What's the matter, afraid people will get bored? Huh? Thought this one was for you? Thought you were going to write yourself out of the corner? Did we mention suicidal thoughts? The ones that started a couple of years ago? How easily we forget. Come on, Felicity. You remember the day you and Spouse were having a nice drive in the countryside and you asked him to pull over because you had a sudden and very strong urge to open the door and hurl yourself out onto the road? Actually, not hurl. Your impulse had been to just sort of roll out sideways and let hitting the tarmac at fifty miles an hour do the rest.

What Felicity hadn't been able to understand then was that the desire to die in that moment was so ultimate, so matter-of-fact, and yet one second later the desire to live had her urging Spouse to stop the car. Well, it had been a hell of a year.

It was their second year living full-time on the farm. The first year of living in a foreign land in a foreign tongue had been energizing, for both of them. Spouse had started a new, completely different body of work and Felicity had finally written the novel she had first conceived of some fourteen years earlier.

Fourteen years earlier, while giving a public reading of a short story she'd written, it suddenly seemed not to be a short story at all but rather the opening chapter of a novel. So the next day, sitting at her desk in the tiny shed on Cape Cod, she had begun chapter two. Six characters appeared to her and the idea of them arguing their individual beliefs while trapped overnight in an isolated Cornish inn seemed rich with possibility. Especially since time-wise she was setting the novel right before the turn of the millennium when hopes were high and positive and all of us were ignorant of how soon such hope would be destroyed; first by the U.S. Supreme Court electing an ignoramus over an intelligent man to become the president, then came 9/11 and the last vestige of belief that America was a safe haven would be brutally demolished; then the economic crash and now, the erroneous election of a mentally deranged, narcissistic, lying racist to the presidency. So, yes. Felicity had thought to put the reader back in time with a set of beliefs that, with the exception of one, would soon be proven laughable. Yes, she had thought, this is a great idea for a novel, except that when she got to the end of chapter two, she had had the horrendous realization that it would take a better writer than her to do it justice. And so she had quietly put it in the drawer.

Then, fourteen years later, during their first summer on the farm, finally returned to Europe with the man she loved, in the midst of peace and beauty, she was finally ready to embark on that novel. For six months she was on fire and when the first draft was complete she sent it off to a freelance editor who had been highly recommended, someone known in London literary circles. Someone who believed Felicity's novel had a good chance out in the world. Someone who would help her finesse it until it became the best it could possibly be, and finally, someone who would put it in the hands of an agent.

Spouse thought it her best work, as did all the readers she gave it to for critique. But most important, Felicity believed in it. So what fucking wonderful irony, that her belief was dashed along with those of her characters. Synopsis, bio, author's photo, and manuscript rejected by one agent after another. Promises of help from acquaintances in the biz evaporating like small talk at a cocktail party. What the hell! One agent had actually written that she "loooved" the novel but had just accepted a similar manuscript by another writer. Really? Are you fucking kidding me? You mean there's another writer out there who's written a novel about six characters trapped in a Cornish inn in November 1999 examining the validity of their beliefs? There is rejection and then there is rejection. Once again, Felicity falls to her knees while Spouse's star soars higher than ever. Once again, Felicity has to try and climb out of the ditch while making lunch for editors who actually come to the farm asking to publish books of Spouse's art and accompanying text. Oh, fucking glory, what do you think? Of course she's angry. Tell me, Felicity wants to scream, how to make whole the division between happiness for Spouse and seething resentment that he doesn't even have to ask for acceptance? It's a given. And yes, she will smile at openings and parties at galleries and museums as she introduces herself, because if she doesn't, who will? And yes, she will burn with shame and fury at the many dinners when guests will politely ask her, "And what do you do?" She will tell them, even though she knows that the follow up question will be the end of her.

"I'm a writer."

"Oh, how interesting. Who's your publisher?"

It's a while yet before Felicity will answer, "Me. I am the publisher."

She will watch as she is once again dismissed. So, yes, there is such a thing as compound rejection. Yes, there is such a thing as exponential fury and self-withering resentment. And fuck all who enter here, because this is Felicity's world. This is the soul-destroying, physically exhausting, mentally disturbing, stupid decision she makes over and over again. No, she doesn't take it on the chin? Are you kidding? She takes it in the core of her being, that hole at the center of her existence that resounds with rejection. And yet, goddamn it, up she gets, a little slower now, a little bloodier, but she's still in the ring and she will not be counted out.

34

AND FELICITY HAS BEEN IN THE RING. The first time she put her dukes up she beat the shit out of the little fucker.

It was the day after she handed over her three-year-old daughter to the father. She was, and had been on and off, in love with a drummer boy. She called him her gypsy. Italian-American. Seven years her junior. He'd brought his conga drum to dance class one day and as he played he never took his eyes off Felicity as she leaped and twirled and arched and thrust her pelvis into the beat. She would catch flashes of him, his hands coaxing the drum; long fingers fluttering in a blur of movement. Jazz and Latin rhythms transmitted from his skin through the drum's skin into hers. His dark, dark eyes, softened, as they were, by the ridiculously long black lashes. He was one of the magical men. Of course, they became lovers. Of course, his magic was never for her alone. Magic has no boundaries, no rules, no loyalty. And he was a coward, too. Had followed her to San Francisco like a lost puppy and she'd fallen for him all over again.

But when he stood her up on the day of the custody hearing, when she had waited at the bus stop until the last minute before boarding the bus alone, entering the courthouse alone, losing custody alone, taking her child to the Ice Capades alone, watching, alone, as her little girl ran across the wooden bridge to her daddy, standing there alone, then getting on the bus to nowhere and threatening a stranger who dared look at her, that may not have been the day she first became angry, but it was certainly the day she became capable of physical violence. The next day, when drummer boy tried to pull the sheepish trick, she had grabbed him by his shirt and thrown him against the wall. She can hear him now, pleading with her, "Oh babe, oh come on babe, please," and she's racing down the seedy stairs out on to the street and he keeps following her and pleading and she turns on him, spits in his face, kicks him, slapping him about the head. She hears construction workers jeering as she punches his pretty face and she feels murderous hatred for every one of them. She turns to them, screaming, "What's the matter, you fucking assholes? Ya scared?" The workers stand there, three of them, one story up on scaffolding, beer bellies protruding through their grimy BVD vests, the type of vests that will soon be called wife-beaters. They are coarse and hairy and big and they are cowards and Felicity hauls off and slaps drummer boy into the chain link fence and walks away.

That night she begins her career in cocaine and alcohol. She would much rather die, but like that crack mother whose baby she will one day deliver, she loves her own too much to die. She lives because she hopes that one day she will get a second chance to be her daughter's mother. But the pain of losing her is a bloodless wound and in order to survive she must numb it.

She's the only straight woman on a staff of thirty gay male waiters at Hamburger Mary's, down there in the Mission. She's the cocktail waitress, which she finds ironic, because in this place she will neither be tail nor get cock. She starts the gig a week after she loses custody and a week later she will move into the shabby one-room apartment over the restaurant. Within weeks she will be scoring the coke for the evening shift. They will nickname her apartment the Snow-Kissed Lounge. On the wooden crates that serve as her coffee table, a large round mirror will hold a dozen ten-dollar lines of cocaine, each line forming the initial that corresponds with the names of the waiters who have prepaid. And all evening the swing door to the restaurant rotates one waiter after another out on to the street and up one flight to the mirror, the door swinging faster as each waiter reenters, picks up an order from the kitchen and dances it to the customers' table.

Felicity saves her lines until after the shift, and then at 2 a.m., she will snort them and drink coffee laced with brandy while she works on her legal brief. She lost the case in San Francisco because of a technical detail of which no lawyer had bothered to inform her. Because the joint custody agreement that she and Spouse Number Two had signed a year earlier had taken place in New York State, it was decreed that the case must be tried in that state. Because at that time Spouse Number Two was the New York State resident, while Felicity was now a California resident, by law the child must be given to the New York parent until the case came to trial there. Yes, just as with medical care, there are different levels of justice depending on who your lawyer is. Spouse Number Two can afford the unscrupulous attorney who also plays golf with the judge who will preside over the case. The lawyer will contrive to keep the court hearing off the calendar for nine months, giving Spouse Number Two the advantage of having had the child live with him long enough for it to be deemed damaging to uproot said child. And this lawyer will barefacedly lie to the judge that he was in the room when Spouse Number Two gave Felicity his newly unlisted number . . . and therefore it will be shown that Felicity is negligent, in that she has not called her daughter once during those nine months. Well of course she bloody well hadn't . . . she'd never been given the fucking number.

But we digress. It's still her first night at Hamburger Mary's. "There's a call for you in the office, honey," one of the waiters informs her before pirouetting off to a nearby table carrying the best hamburgers and fries in the city of San Francisco. "Line one," he calls over his shoulder. The men have all fallen safely in love with her. She goes back to the office, picks up the phone, presses line one and hears a dial tone. Confused, she returns to the bar. "There was no one there," she says. The bartender laughs, comes out from the bar, and takes her by the hand back to the office. He points to a mirror on the desk. Two thin lines lie side by side. The bartender takes a length of straw from his back pocket, "Like this," he says, and Felicity watches as the powder disappears in a snort. He hands her the straw, pouting his lips like a coquette, "Line one, darling." And there she goes. Hook, line, and sinker.

35

SO SHE TRASHES the literary death book, the ice cream melts, they have tuna for lunch, she gets married, separates, fucks the director, goes to the nuthouse, marries again, has a stillborn daughter . . . oh, she's not written about that yet? Well, not now. Now it's time for a recap and, she wishes, a nightcap or two. She's desperately searching for humor here. God forbid she should scare the reader, or worse, bore her. There you go again, Felicity, always looking for acceptance. On you go. Dead baby, then a live baby, same father, loses that one in the custody battle, beats up the boyfriend, marries and divorces Numbers Three and Four and breaks her neck. Slow down, her mother warns, one of these days you'll break your neck. Mothers always know.

Back in San Francisco, it's New Year's Eve at Hamburger Mary's, maybe 1977. The waiters are on roller skates, decked to the nines, or in Russell's case, draped in his mother's Christmas gift to him: a circular, green felt tablecloth, its border appliqued in sequined brocade, the scallops of which are regularly interrupted by red felt Santas and cotton-ball snowmen. Russell has ingeniously cut a round hole in the middle of this tablecloth and elasticized it into a waistband. He staggers through the swing door on his skates and executes a wobbly spin, the skirt flaring up and out to expose legs coiffed in red hair.

Felicity's mirror has been brought down to the office, roller skates not being conducive to a flight of stairs, even if a few of the *girls* do fancy themselves Ginger Rogers. The shift will pass in manic gaiety. There's a lot of leather tonight; the ubiquitous motorcycle jackets, tight pants, vests opened to reveal chained nipples, leather chaps exposing hairy butts, S&M versions of yodel pants, and, of course, Nazi caps. Then there are the ladies, the Chers and Marilyns and Joans and Bettes, all of them laden with tiers of false eyelashes beneath sparkly lids, the outrageously outlined lips, the evening gowns, and shaved cleavage, size eleven platforms and glued-on nails. The cook may as well have stayed home, who's eating? Apart from a slice or two of carrot cake for the Marijuana Millies, most of the clientele stifle appetites with coke and poppers, slaking their thirst with gaudy cocktails that Felicity carries on tray after tray, the fruit and paper umbrellas poised above liquids of venomous psychedelic hues, and yes, there's LSD, too. Felicity holding the tray high on the arched fingers of her right hand while she pinches buttocks with her left, singing, "Coming through, coming through." She sees her child on tippy toes, smelling the blossoms on the lilac tree in the backyard of the house she and Spouse Number Two bought while Felicity was pregnant and asks the bartender to top up her French coffee. It's Walter tonight. She has a crush on him. Everyone does. He refers to himself as a haughty nigger and indeed he is a supercilious queen. But his sexiness beckons everyone alike.

Felicity will end the night at the Top of the Mark, with Walter and Russell and a couple of other waiters. One of them, like Felicity, is an ex-modern dancer and the two of them will dazzle the patrons with a *pas de deux* of heartbreaking longing. And when a well-known Hollywood actor enters with a starlet on his arm, Russell will score one for the offense, lifting his felt tablecloth to reveal his naked sex, the sight of which will cause a sneer on the actor's face before his swiveled exit.

Felicity has no recollection of how or when she gets home. But she vividly remembers seeing the shit stain on her duvet. Evidently a couple of the "girls" weren't wearing skates.

Felicity caps her pen. The kids are due in two hours. She wonders if Karl Ove Knausgård had a sense of humor in his memoir or was it all just struggle, struggle, struggle.

36

OH, COME ON, FELICITY. It hasn't all been struggle, has it? Think of all the ecstasy. In fact, why don't you just back up a bit. Maybe more than a bit. That's it. Today is your third birthday, remember?

Felicity and her parents have gone by coach to Ilfracombe, in those days, a modest seaside town on the exquisite northwest coast of Devon. Her first memory of the journey is of standing on the seat next to her mother who has stripped her down to her little petticoat, Felicity having vomited down the smocked bodice of her Sunday-best dress. Dad is standing in the aisle waiting for the mopping up to be finished. Felicity's brother is not with them . . . perhaps he is at boy scout camp. The next thing Felicity remembers is waking up in a small hotel. It is her birthday. In the dining room, breakfast is being served. There are perhaps a dozen tables and the guests at those nearest to Felicity are clucking and tut-tutting about what a big girl she is. Felicity, at that age, has not been completely repressed, although she has already experienced the existence of shame thanks to her mother's tutelage. Still, she is a lovely mix of exuberance and shyness, the former quality accounting for her having informed those within earshot that she is three years old today. There are several "well, I never," and "aren't you the lucky girl," utterances interrupting the gentile beheading of soft-boiled eggs and the scrape of butter over dry toast.

When Felicity and her parents return for dinner that evening the gift of a toy dustpan and brush is presented to Felicity by the ancient couple at the table to her left. A cake arrives, its three candles flicker over the icing like moonlight on a frozen pond. Hypnotized, Felicity watches them the way she will be held rapt by firelight as an adult. She wants them to stay lit forever, but her mother is telling her to hurry up and blow them out. Felicity is distraught. Why would anyone want to extinguish such magic? "Stop sniveling," says her mother, "cry on your birthday, you'll cry for seven years." So Felicity obeys and all the guests clap. She files this information away: performance equals applause. Now, where there were bright flames, three little wisps of smoke drift and disperse. The guests go back to their dinner while Felicity sits bereft of light and attention. But the cake beckons, the icing a sweet buzz in her tiny mouth, and what fun to sweep up the crumbs with her dustpan and brush.

The next day Daddy will show her the magic of a double sunset. They have spent the day on the beach and now the sun is falling, falling. "Look," Daddy says, and together they watch as the golden ball disappears behind a dune. Felicity feels the same sadness she felt when she blew out the candles. More than sadness, she feels a terrible loss. She begins to cry. Her father takes her hand and together they climb to the top of the dune and hey, there is the sun again! Now it's sinking into the sea. The air is chilly, the color fading from the water.

"No," she cries, "don't go!"

"It's OK," Daddy says, "it'll be back tomorrow."

There the seed of addiction is planted; the idea that there is always more of a good thing to be had if you just hang with the right people in the right place at the right time. For the rest of the holiday, Felicity will insist on two sunsets every evening. Sugar Daddy.

Ah, yes. Daddy. She still longs for him. Now she longs for him to know where she has arrived in her life. Even though she is suffering inexplicable, shame-inducing negativity, she is also proud of how far she has come and how much she has overcome. She thinks it would please him to see this. And pleasing him was something she was continually trying to do as a child.

What was it about him that made her want him, as opposed to her mother, whom she wished would just go away? Strange that she had intuitively known from early, early on that there was no biological connection between her and her mother. And yet, her father, in spite of his remoteness, always felt unquestionably to be her father.

Felicity looks at the clock hoping it will show that there's not enough time before the kids arrive for her to delve into what she knows will be a bottomless pool of sadness, his and her own. She feels the urge to cap her pen. But time is not on her side in that there is still another hour and half before she will shine it on for the kids.

Spouse is in his studio. The river still flows eleven stories down and one block over. The sun is licking the wall over the couch where she sits, a luscious glow of golden orange that Felicity would like to bask in. Fuck memories. Fuck fathers.

Maybe it was the actor in him that constantly projected sad romance, the wounded hero. His magnetism was brutal, unavoidable. A force field that pulled her to him in constant adoration. There she is, at the bottom of the ladder watching him paint the eaves of the house. She tries to engage him, but he's far away. There she is at his feet, looking up at him from the fireside rug he hooked on a recent hospital stay. She watches his feet, crossed at the ankles. They are in constant conversation with each other, his feet, wiggling back and forth as he rolls a cigarette. Golden Flake. Manly hands. She's in love with his thumbs. He licks the paper, seals it over the tobacco and lights the slender tube that is already feeding the cancer he will die of when Felicity is twenty-three and far from home. She looks up at those eyes, a cliché shade of Paul Newman blue. She's sure that if she keeps looking at him, he will turn to her, smile, reach for her. But it never happens. Yet she can, to this day, feel her hand in his. And when they hold hands, they are the aliens, not to each other, but from the rest of world, creatures related by alchemy and tribe. Like when he holds her hand and shows her the double sunset. And again, when he holds her hand on her fifth birthday.

Her mother has complained about him all day, telling little Felicity how it's all left up to her, that he does nothing to acknowledge that it's her birthday. And with every complaint the child winces. Can it be true that she is of no consequence to him? He's coming in the garden gate. She hears the click of the latch. She wants to run to him but mother tells her to go upstairs and wash her hands. When she comes back down her parents stop talking and Daddy says, "How about I take you to the sweet shop for your birthday present?" She can barely breathe. He takes her hand and they walk up the lane to the main road. She's excited about the chocolate, but more than that she loves the feel of his hand holding hers. Such different sizes they are and yet the fit is perfect. Of course, she doesn't have the words, but she feels she belongs, right there in the palm of his hand. Do they talk as they walk? Does she chatter and he listen? In her memory, they walk in silence. The sun is shining. It's five-thirty on an August evening. In the sweet shop he shows her the different chocolate bars from which she may choose. Choose? Her mother never lets her choose. While she is trying to decide, Daddy lets go of her hand to pick up the evening paper. She feels the loss. She chooses quickly and reaches for his hand. He tucks the newspaper under his arm and together they walk home, one hand holding his, the other clutching the bar of chocolate.

Memories of her father are few and confusing. She longs for him the way all little girls long for their daddies, but apart from that birthday, and a couple of other times when they find themselves together without her mother, the memories are of unrequited love, and later, when she is a teenager, there will be scathing judgment of each other. Yet now, as the sun disappears into the murk of New Jersey, a series of stop-action scenes scroll across her memory. In all of them her father is isolated, distant, sad. Sadness and loneliness enshrouded him. Even when he was onstage he emanated tortured sorrow. Now he sits by the fire, ankles crossed, feet stilled, a half-rolled cigarette paused between fingers and thumbs. Something on television has taken him even further away and little Felicity, sitting on the floor beside him, watches as streams of tears run down his cheeks.

For years, as an adult, Felicity will dream of him. The same dream, several times each year. He is always alone, walking down a corridor, his back to her. In the dream, Felicity runs to catch up with him, slips her hand in his, and awakens.

When Felicity is eleven, her father is relocated to the north of England for his work. Her mother, a working-class snob, refuses to leave the fashionable, genteel town on the south coast. By now, Felicity's brother is long gone. Each year the army takes him further away: Gibraltar, Cypress, Jerusalem. Now it's just Felicity and her mother. Once a month her dad makes the long journey down from Liverpool to Bournemouth. Felicity has no memory of these weekends. Her father and brother are ghosts, lost to her.

One weekend, after he has come and gone, there is an indescribable feeling in the house. Her mother is agitated. Angry. She comes to the foot of Felicity's bed. "Your father's found another woman."

Felicity finds this news exciting. At the same time, she is keenly aware that she must take her mother's side. Evidently, a powder compact and a woman's name and address have been discovered over the weekend, the two pieces of evidence lying secretly in the inside pocket of Dad's raincoat. Her mother is seething. "After all I've done for him," she says.

Within weeks the house is sold, Felicity is torn from school, from friends, from piano lessons, from the hawthorn tree outside her bedroom window, there where the summer birds gather to serenade her into dreamland. Gone the click of the gate latch, gone the six in the morning whistle of the milkman, the clink of the bottles as he puts them outside the front door. Gone her friend Patricia, next door. Gone the moss-topped stone walls she runs her hand along on the lazy walk home from school. Gone the corner sweet shop, the bus to the sea, the smell of dried ferns she and the neighborhood kids fashioned into their summer hideaway. Gone the crook in her favorite oak tree, where she would sit above the world, eating sweeties. Gone her friend Jill and weekend sleepovers at her house. Gone the green brocade bedroom curtains in which she discovered faces and forests and secret places, staring into their drawn folds before sleep. Gone the raspberries and gooseberries, the apples, the vegetable patch, and the greenhouse. Gone the rhubarb patch and the chance to pick a couple of them for use as pretend umbrellas. Gone the rag 'n' bone man; the onion man who ferried over from Brittany, his handlebars dangling strings of them, their crinkly skins rustling in the midday sun. The Sunday walk along Mustcliffe Lane to see the cows and horses and swans. Gone. Singing Christmas carols in the dark on neighborhood doorsteps. Gone. Gone the Kingfisher Troop of the Girl Guides. Gone the Saturday morning winter swims in the Winton indoor pool. Gone the no-hands bike rides, licking a raspberry ice-lolly. Gone the message to her brother she's inscribed in the wet cement of the garden path. No more visits to the wild horses of the New Forest. Her father will never sit in coat and trilby on the deserted autumn beach while Felicity takes the last swim of the year. Her brother won't be home for Christmas. The lodgings in Liverpool will be meager and foreign and Felicity will notice that her mother places the bolster down the middle of the bed each night. She will not let another woman have him after all she's put up with. But neither will she let him have her. Eventually the three of them will move into a new two-bedroom bungalow. Her father will plant potatoes in the bare earth of the back garden to enrich the soil. Her brother, home on leave, will give her a puppy and a turquoise three-speed bike. It will be three years before she escapes the cruelty that has become home. She will learn to smoke. She will learn to hate her parents. She will despise her father's cowardice. She will do badly in school. She will be chastised by her father and hit by her mother and she will continue to dream and believe and endure the torturous swings of adolescence, the burgeoning spirit of freedom, the possibility of love, the desire for fame, the desolation of a loveless home, the shame of small breasts, the joy of athletic prowess, the sadism of a jealous teacher, the ecstasy of a wet tongue in the mouth, the fear of cum in her hand, the soul-destroying cruelty of not being allowed to go to art college, love letters stolen, the shock of her mother's hands around her neck, the sweet loss of her virginity on the next-door neighbor's fireside rug, the brutality of the early morning train to work at the Vernon's Football Pools, the hot blade of her first whisky knifing her between the shoulders and, finally, the train to London.

37

SUFFICE IT TO SAY there are three adult children and a couple of grandkids. But they're off limits. Sorry, but Felicity feels that her anger is not their fault, nor their problem. She and Spouse did not make these children together and they are not, as the ridiculous phrase goes, a blended family; the children being too old by the time Felicity and Spouse met to have any need or desire to have another go at Happy Families. So, let's just say the visit was fine and the dinner tasty.

Oh, to hell with it. OK, dinner was fine, but the visit? Who knows how it was for the kids? For Felicity, it was another exercise in evaluating every thought before verbalizing it, or not. Better to just shut up most of the time and avoid judgment. And yes, she's angry about that. How old will she have to be before she's forgiven? Yes, she fucked up and she can't ever make up for that. Ever. But do twenty-nine years of sober mothering do nothing to make amends for the first sixteen years? Maybe when she's sober thirty-two years it will be enough. Two good years for every bad one?

They didn't stay long. Those with kids of their own doing their best to fulfill the responsibilities of good parenting: homework, brushing of teeth, a bedtime story for the youngest. Felicity used to think that when her kid had a kid things would change. But that's not on the books anymore and besides, there are plenty of kids who become parents and still have no compassion for their own. So there you go. Game over. Two chances at it: one dead on arrival and the other lost in a custody battle and to alcohol. How the hell could that really be her story? How could she have squandered the thing she had most wanted: to love and be loved by her own child?

"How you doing?" Spouse asks as they finish loading the dishwasher.

"I'm okay," she says, wiping down the table. "They're okay, don't you think?" she adds, referring to the kids.

"They seem to be fine," Spouse says and chuckles.

"What's funny?"

"Well, it's all relative isn't it?" he says. "I mean, fine compared to what? When they were teenagers? Sure. Compared to us at their age? Mostly. Compared to other people's kids? Superior without doubt."

Jesus, why is he always so damn positive? For someone capable of scathing criticism when it comes to the art world how can he be so blind to the rest of life? Is he blind? Or was the man born with rose-tinted vision? She wants to lash out, but is too exhausted. Instead, she just goes along with him. "Superior indeed," she says, and heads back to the couch. She closes her eyes and immediately feels a deep disturbance, more visceral than mental. As though something is gathering deep in her. Something that wants out. Something green and nasty. Is bile actually green? What color is anger? How does green become red? She's on the delivery table. Which one? The one delivering death, or life? Her legs are spread, the doctor's head a capped blob between them. Both labors are excruciating. But the first is filled with hours of horror having been told the baby is dead inside her. Three days before the first is born, vile green discharge plops itself into her knickers. Of course, her obstetrician is on vacation. The one covering for him laughs it off. Months later, a friend training to become an obstetrician tells her that that type of discharge is called pea-soup discharge and is a sign of fetal distress. The autopsy will show that the baby died a few hours after Felicity called the doctor. Bloody doctors. So sorry to interrupt your golf-game with fetal distress. Talk about teed off, you have no fucking idea. It's nineteen seventy-one. A stillbirth equals a failed cake. A burned bun in the oven. Go home and make another one. Throw this one away and whip up a new one. There, there, never mind. We'll just cut this one up, see what went wrong and then toss it out. To this day Felicity sees her baby in pieces in a garbage bag. A dissected, desiccated life, binned. Oh, she's just getting started now, motherfuckers.

Call it irony. Felicity calls it cruelty. The child dies on its due date. The due date arrives and passes. On the second night, her belly starts to pull over to one side. What does she know? It's her first pregnancy. Are these contractions? At four in the morning, Spouse Number Two drives them the hour and half to the hospital in Manhattan. Felicity lays on the back seat. They are about to become parents. She watches the night lighten, watches the dawn pink the sky. Watches lush trees rush by. Their baby is on its way.

She knows before she is told. First the cold disc of the stethoscope searching her belly. Poor intern. He leaves the room. Comes back with a doctor who turns on the ultrasound machine. Again, the taut skin is searched. Felicity hears the gurgles and swishes of her belly. But no heartbeat. No heartbeat. No heartbeat. Someone says, "I'm afraid your baby's in distress." What a coward. Of course, she's in distress. She's dead! Again she's left alone. Perhaps, she thinks, the baby is hiding. Or the machine isn't working properly. Or there's a leak in the stethoscope. Come on, Amy. Come out, come out, wherever you are. It will be five hours before she comes out. Felicity lies alone wondering when she can go home. She wants to goes home. And then, the awful, awful realization that she still has to give birth. To death.

They induce her labor, to get it over and done with, but it will never be over. Maybe, Felicity thinks, once her baby comes out the fresh air will do her good. Spouse Number Two stands by the side of the bed, an oxymoron of present absence. The nightmare has only just begun and it is all hers. Back labor. Five hours. Excruciating physical and mental pain. She wants to die. Leave the baby there and let me die. They don't allow Spouse Number Two into the delivery room. Natch. Protect the men from reality at all costs. She is deeply alone and longing to see her child. She is pushing, pushing, pushing. Perhaps if she pushes hard enough the heart will beat. Come on, Amy. We can do it. She feels something leave her like a sigh. She sits up to reach for her baby, to hold her, to see her, to love her, to nurse her. Instead, she sees the interior of a gas mask. All done. When she comes to she's being asked to sign something. Later she finds out it was an autopsy form. As she's being wheeled through the maternity ward a baby cries and her milk lets down and for weeks after, in supermarket aisles, on the street, watching TV, every time a baby cries milk will leak from her in search of a mouth and there, in the shape that arms make in order to hold an infant, Felicity will feel a howling emptiness.

38

FELICITY HASN'T WRITTEN for months. Turns out she was quite ill. Following the advice given the night of her collapse in New York, she went to see one of those newfangled integrated medicine doctors. What the hell that means she had no idea, nor did she trust it much. Integrative medicine? Integrated with what? Quinoa? Anyway, she bled into fourteen vials, pissed into tiny plastic cups, shat in a box before scooping some of it into a bottle with a cute little plastic spoon, giving new meaning to playing with one's food. A nonintegrated, noninteractive technician daubed jelly—no peanut butter—onto her throat, chest, and abdomen before running his nonmagical wand over those areas in order to divine the state of her thyroid, heart, and intestines. The combined results of these tests read like ticker tape on the verge of a Dow Jones crash. Thyroid: a dessicated butterfly no longer able to produce or convert the necessary hormones. Elevated cholesterol, weight loss, dangerously low cortisol, ditto vitamins D and B12. High level of ammonia. Blood pressure eight-four over fifty-eight. The doctor, integrating four hundred bucks into his wallet every thirty minutes while pedaling on the treadmill under his desk, never once laid hands on her, which, for fuck's sake, is the one scenario where it is not only all right for a man to do so, but is, in fact, desirable.

But give the man his due. What he was able to learn and impart from these results was that Felicity's endocrine and immune systems had been in decline for several years and this decline had caused the following smorgasbord:

1. Exhaustion
2. Joint pain
3. Allergic rashes
4. Diarrhea
5. Leg cramps
6. Depression
7. Brain fog
8. Anxiety
9. Insomnia
10. Acid reflux

"Basically," he said, "you've been in fight or flight mode for a couple of years or so." No kidding! Two years? How about seventy?

He sent her back to Europe with supplements and minerals, thyroid medication and B12 shots and, over the course of the following few months, all that had been ailing her on the list, one through ten, gradually started disappearing. Now she is gardening without pain and sleeping through the night. Now she is no longer in panic or overwhelmed. Cramps? Gone. Suicidal thoughts? Gone. Brain fog, diarrhea, exhaustion? All gone.

Suddenly, she is feeling the way she felt after she broke her neck; grateful to be alive, accepting of reality, energetic but not manic.

She watches herself daily in amazement, if slightly on the alert for any sign that her well-being might diminish without warning.

"It's so good to have you back," Spouse says, as they prepare dinner together.

"It's good to be back," she says. And it is. Except there is a bit of a problem that Felicity isn't willing to share at the moment. There is something else that has disappeared along with all the other symptoms. Something that hadn't been on the doctor's list. Anger. And, come to think of it, resentment. Oh, and ambition. These days Felicity doesn't really care that Spouse is famous and she is not. She no longer gives a toss about achieving success, or rather she has redefined it. Why, she had finally asked herself, had she spent so much time and energy trying to get approval from people whose values she abhorred? So, well done, Felicity. Yeah, but . . . now what?

How is she supposed to write herself out of the corner when there no longer is one? How is she supposed to finish writing a novel about an angry woman now that she is no longer angry? She lets it go. For a while. But then she starts to feel a bit pissed off. It's one thing to write a novel and have it rejected, but quite another to have one killed off in its prime. Until she was diagnosed she felt she was really getting somewhere in her search for the seed of her rage and now suddenly it seems to have come to a screeching halt, or not even, more like a fuse she lit all those months ago ended in a damp squib and fizzled out. It's not that she misses the anger. She just doesn't understand where it went, any more than she understands where it came from.

But surely, Felicity, the search is not over, because really, what you have here is a classic chicken-and-egg scenario. The question here is did you become angry because you were ill, or ill because you were angry for so long that you inflamed your system almost to the point of self-immolation?

Felicity asks Spouse would he mind doing the dishes?

"Of course not," he says, turning to her with a look of concern. "Are you all right?"

"Yes," she says, "I just feel like writing for a bit."

"Go to it!" he says, relief and genuine happiness for her spreading across his face.

And off she goes, up to her desk, where she uncaps her pen and begins to hunt for the egg.

39

FELICITY SITS FOR A LONG TIME, struggling with apathy, if apathy is something with which one can struggle. She spends some time parsing this; surely apathy is as complete a state of being as is depression, a state in which there is no air, no crack, no window, and certainly no door through which to exit? Apathy is an hermetically sealed chamber in which one finds oneself not so much unwilling as lacking the desire to change one's circumstances, be it personal or political. Zero interest in anything. In this moment, Felicity has zero interest in continuing to write whatever this thing is that she's been inking on and off for all these months. Now, devoid of anger, she feels cheated of its energy. In the rest of her life, she's feeling energetic and mainly content. As a writer she feels flaccid. Now, living pain-free and free of all the other physical symptoms, she wonders if the price for good health is lack of creative drive. She's actually beginning to feel a bit pissed off. She had so much more to say.

It's mid-June, a sweet early summer evening. The window's open to the old oak trees out back. Two mourning doves call back and forth to each other: three notes apiece; the notes identical with a slight hesitation between the second and third. Oh, and hang on a minute, is the third note a little lower on the scale? Another dove joins in. Same story. And now another. Same notes, same rhythm, although this one sounds slightly adamant. For how many centuries has this species been uttering the same notes? And to whom? To one another or the world at large? Who is listening? What are they in mourning for? There goes that adamant one again, not exactly a screech, but vociferous, maybe a tad impatient. Felicity is riveted, straining to hear beneath the repetitive notes as if some cry is being uttered over and over in the hope that one day it will finally be heard.

The birds stop all of a sudden, done for the day. But they'll be back tomorrow with the same old cry. In the silence, Felicity hears the cry of women. The same old story. Three notes: Set us free, set us free, set us free. Suddenly Felicity understands that much of her anger is part of this universal cry. Sure the details are personal but don't they derive from the same source?

Now what is she to do? Drop everything and change course? For the first time in a couple of months, she feels overwhelmed, feels like she is embarking on a subject too big for her skills. But instantly she knows that's a cop-out. And she knows that if she puts this one in the drawer it will stay there forever. What would be so bad about that? Could she not let go and finally live in peace for whatever time she has left? God, what a relief that would be. But a life once examined cannot be covered over. Felicity knows that while she may have written herself out of the corner, she is now out in the open and if she runs for cover she will not only be a failed writer but a failed human being. A woman lacking the courage to go the distance.

If you thought you were alone in your anger, join the crowd, Felicity. Get on your soapbox and join the chorus. And know this, as you step up onto its rickety surface, there will be cheers and jeers, obscenities will be hurled along with rotting food and excrement and the threat of rape and death. Men will become defensive, abusive, murderous. Do you have the courage of women like Mary Beard, who actually chooses to engage with evil trolls who use the Internet to tell her they're going to cut off her head and shove it up her cunt? Are you prepared to face the denial of women who are not yet willing to examine the ways in which they perpetuate, contribute, in some cases even instigate the very behavior they decry in men? Are you ready, Felicity, to allow your story to be only one among the billions over millennia? Are you willing to have your tongue cut out and still, like Philomela, determined to be heard, go weave the tapestry that depicts the story of that vile act? How many words, how many stitches, how many repetitive notes will it take to incorporate your story into those of women everywhere, no matter where, no matter race, class, creed, or color? And how many deaf ears will be turned? How many young boys' ears will be covered by the hands of fathers determined not to cede authority, superiority, and majority rule?

Good luck to you, Felicity. You just wrote your way onto the very stage you've avoided your entire life. Get up there and take your rightful place, up there with Eve and Mary and King Solomon's wife; with Medusa and Rapunzel and Philomela; with the Brontë Sisters and Colette and George Eliot; up there with the suffragettes, who repeatedly went to jail, fasted, were force-fed; the feeding tube sometimes shoved into the windpipe, the gruel clogging lungs, while others were trampled to death by horses whose baton-wielding white men showed who was in charge. Are you ready to stand with Betty Friedan, Gloria Steinem, yeah, and Hillary, and bear the ridicule and chants of "Lock her up." Go on, get up there with Oprah, Sojourner Truth, Joan of Arc, Joan Didion. Shoulder to shoulder with Edna O'Brien, her first published novel burned in her homeland. Simone de Beauvoir, Eleanor Roosevelt,

Alice Walker, Ruth Bader Ginsburg. Malala Yousafzai, shot in the head at age fifteen for standing up for her right to an education. Do you have the balls of Bella Abzug, the steely determination of Madeleine Albright? Come on, Felicity, join the queue. There's Maya Angelou, another silenced woman who found her voice. Stand next to her and say hello to Margaret Atwood, Susan Brownmiller, Nawal El Sadaawi, Margaret Sanger, Virginia Woolf, Chimamanda Ngozi Adichie, and Martina Navratilova.

As she writes these names, she begins to feel embarrassed about how little she really knows about the history of women. Damn it, she thinks, I'm going to have to do some serious research. She almost laughs at the self-indulgent irritation she feels at being interrupted by two thousand years of women's inequality. Wants to just write her way past this because, damn it, wasn't she just having some kind of revelation about her own inequality?

So what's the big deal, Felicity? Just leave a space here and go back to it when you've finished the first draft. She's suddenly a bit excited at the prospect of research, begins to envision herself pouring over tomes in various libraries; women's libraries, feminist libraries, maybe even the British Library. Wow. Awesome, such an incredible place. Yeah, and she could ask her daughter for input. Perfect. Her daughter, the ardent feminist and women's studies major. They could brainstorm together. Felicity can already see the acknowledgments page: "*With heartfelt thanks to my daughter, without whose knowledgeable help and generosity* . . ." blah, blah, blah. For fuck's sake, Felicity, why don't you write your Booker acceptance speech while you're at it? Why would you even want the damn thing anyway? You who decry the arse-licking protocol of such awards?

The truth is, the last thing Felicity wants to do is sit in libraries memorizing the names, dates, and types of cruelty women have endured over the centuries. What would she do with such research?

Write a dissertation to prove how academically endowed she is and then stick the damn thing in right here and bore the tits off everyone? Whatever it is you're writing, Felicity, it ain't a doctoral thesis.

She takes a breath, relieved to have let herself off *that* particular hook and instead looks back over the list of women she's just enumerated and feels a profound belonging. Yet as much as it feels comforting, it also saddens her. She doesn't really want to be in the "us versus them" position. All her adult life, she's tried to see the strengths and weakness of both men and women; has in fact argued with women over the years when any number of them have complained that there are hardly any good men; has insisted on pointing out that neither are there as many good women as we'd like to think there are . . . whatever the fuck "good" means. If she's honest, Felicity has silently judged many women for choosing to judge men harshly while never taking a look at their own shortcomings. And she still believes this to be true. But in the months that have elapsed since she collapsed, until her recently recovered good health, she has witnessed the undeniable tsunami of women's rage surging across continents, outing once powerful men. Women encouraging each other, holding each other up in order to hold men accountable. She's watched with glee as men have been toppled and banished from their seats of power, even though one of the most abusive of them all still holds the office of president of the United States. Cry rape! Cry rape! Cry rape! Until the cry is heard. As she writes, Felicity begins to seethe.

She was twenty-one when she was raped. For years she told herself it didn't really matter because she'd already enjoyed sex for a few years, so the rape didn't ruin sex for her. But what about the terror for her life that she'd experienced during the hours the sick bastard raped her? One long rape from one in the morning until six in the morning. What about the terror that took over every cell in her being when he put his hand over her mouth, dragged her out of his car and up two flights of stairs into his apartment, locking the door, ripping the phone out of the wall, telling her his parents were Nazis, that she is his prisoner for the rest of her life, that he will buy her new clothes, that she will never see her family and friends again? At what point, as his cock is knifing into her over and over and over, does Felicity realize that the only chance she has of survival is to agree with everything he says, do every awful thing he insists upon, feign orgasms in the absence of his own, begin to believe that she will never get away? At what point does she convince herself it will be OK, that she can make it work, that she will be able to please him forever and thus be able to live?

To hell with all of you, men and women alike, who blame women for being raped, who refuse to understand why women don't tell, or when they do, don't believe them because they waited so long before telling, and if you are one of the women self-righteously declaring you'd never let that happen to you, shame on you, too. Try a little gratitude instead, that you are one of the lucky ones. Or if you are a man, refusing to admit to your own fantasies of rape, wake the fuck up.

So what happened to Felicity back then when the rapist finally fell asleep at six in the morning with his arm over her chest? It took her an hour to inch her way out from under him, cooing to him and stroking the bastard every time he stirred. When her feet touched the floor at seven, she grabbed her bag and ran naked down the stairs and out into the middle of the street waving frantically at an oncoming car. OK, so the man stops. Give him a fucking star. What does he say? "Get in. I don't want to know." What does he do? He drops her off at the office of a cab company. What does the man behind the counter do? Throws a man's shabby, unclaimed raincoat at her and orders one of his drivers to take her home. And, yes, she has to pay the fare.

When she gets home she calls the police station. What does the cop say after he hears her story? "Did he come in you?" And when she answers, "No," what does he say? "Sorry, nothing we can do."

Felicity throws the coat in the garbage, runs a hot bath, lowers her bruised vagina and terrorized being into the water and sobs there until the water turns cold.

40

FELICITY CAPS HER PEN and sits in silence. It's dark now and a chill breeze has entered the house. She gets up from the desk and stands at the open window watching the leaves of the oak tree come to rest as the breeze dies down. She wonders where the mourning doves have gone. A newborn lamb bleats, its pitiful cry piercing the night. Felicity waits for the mother's response but there is no reassuring maternal *baa*. The lamb bleats again—and again there is silence. Felicity sobs; for the motherless lamb, for women, for the great distance between men and women. She feels no sorrow for herself or for the young woman she was when raped. She knows there are worse stories. She was not, after all, buried up to her neck and stoned to death for being raped. She closes the window against the cold night air but knows she cannot shut out the sound of the mourning dove's lament or the lamb's lonely cry any more than she can shut the pages of her manuscript in order to no longer hear her own voice join the chorus of women demanding to be heard. She knows the time has come, but she is afraid; afraid she's not up to it. Afraid to be seen as part of something strident, afraid of the inevitable backlash that will come, afraid of the honesty and courage it will take to continue to love her husband without exonerating him. Not only does she not want to exonerate him, or the other "good" men she knows, she wants them to step up to the plate instead of away from it. No, you are not excused because you didn't rape someone. No, you are not excused because you didn't beat the shit out of a woman. Don't think you can stand there and say, "But I'm not like that, I'm not one of those men." Sorry, but no, you are not exempt from the culture of male domination. You are not excluded from thousands of years of indoctrination, from the message passed down to every male child that you, the male, are more important, stronger, smarter, deserving of more pay for equal work, have the right to decide what a woman does with her body, of sitting at business meetings remaining silent as the lone woman in the room offers her ideas and the next day co-opting those ideas as your own. Oh, so you're one of the good men? Then really be a good man and take a look at the seed of prejudice against women that you carry. And accept this: some seeds lay dormant, buried under the earth for years, but that same seed, given the wrong conditions, grows twisted, pushing its way up and out in malignant growth, blighting all it comes in contact with. Take note, oh good men, who, without thinking, judge women inferior, who pay no attention to women once the bloom is off them, who call women aggressive for acting in exactly the same way that you judge a man to be assertive and courageous. The men who rape are *you* writ large. The only difference is the extent to which you were indoctrinated.

Felicity does not want to have to write of this; knows that in doing so she has just, probably, written herself off as a publishable writer. Bad enough she started writing a memoir disguised as a novel. At least that stood the chance of being wrapped up in a neat bow. But no one, least of all a man, is going to want to read *this*.

You're on your own now, Felicity. Remember, you said you were writing this for you. So what are you afraid of? Oh, you wanted to be so unique, didn't you? You wanted to be the star of your own story. Now, suddenly, your story is not so big is it? But how about this . . . how about being part of a bigger story?

41

BY THE TIME FELICITY GOES DOWNSTAIRS, Spouse has already gone to bed. On the mantelpiece a single candle remains lit, the flame dancing in the disturbed air as Felicity walks toward it thinking to blow it out. Instead, she sits on the old wooden trunk in front of the fireplace and watches as the flame settles down along with her. She sits for how long, fascinated as much by that single flame as she is mesmerized by the flames of winter fires in the hearth below? The longer she sits, the more she feels a kinship with the candle, its singularity an echo of her solitude in the dark quiet of the house. She feels loath to extinguish it, as if to do so will be akin to silencing a voice.

An image arises. A memory from many years ago. It's Christmas Eve mass in a church on Fifth Avenue. The sermon a rare blend of humor and encouragement at the end of which everyone takes a lit candle out onto the street as if the flames are tongues with which to spread the word.

Is this what women are doing now? Going out into the world lit with anger, the flames spreading like wildfire? As if reading her mind, the candle flares sending a dribble of wax down its ivory body, down the brass holder onto the mantle and over the edge and down to the floor. And Felicity wonders how much blood will be spilled in the revolution and how many men will be unjustly scorched and how many women will once again be extinguished?

The chicken and the egg suddenly seemed to Felicity to be a ridiculous riddle, a total waste of time; like asking how the world came into being. Of course, in *that* scenario man created God in order to explain how man was created by God because lord knows men have to have an answer for everything. Chicken and the egg? Who cares? What about the fucking rooster? That's what Felicity wants to know.

Tiredness finally overtakes her. She blows out the candle, and too tired to bother with even brushing her teeth, creeps into the bedroom and lies down beside her own rooster.

There is no moon tonight and so it takes a while for Felicity's eyes to become adjusted to the darkness. She sees the outline of the wardrobe and dresser, the folds in the velvet curtains and turning toward Spouse gradually sees the outline of his head and neck. It is too dark to make out the crosshatching on his skin, but she knows it is there; knows that it is the neck of the man she loves; knows he is not the enemy. She also knows that the rooster in him is in for a revelation or two.

42

THE FIRST REVELATION COMES a few days later. Spouse is to have an opening at his Paris gallery the next month. Felicity no longer attends all of Spouse's openings, knowing from years of experience that they involve days of interviews and press events for him. So now she only accompanies him if it is to a city where she's happy to spend most of the time alone. Paris is one of those cities.

They have found a reasonably priced flat near the Luxembourg Gardens to rent for a week and, as it has an extra bedroom, Felicity has invited one of her friends whose husband will be away on business to come and stay with them.

An e-mail has just arrived inviting Spouse and Felicity to a dinner party to be held in the home of a wealthy collector, the night before the opening.

"What do you think?" Spouse asks.

"Oh, let's go! Hey, but ask him if we can bring Penny, too."

"I'll write to him right now."

"Why don't you just call? It'll be quicker and we have to leave for the dentist office in a few minutes."

Spouse, to her knowledge, has never written a brief e-mail. In fact, his missives are renowned for being lengthy and overly informative. If only Felicity had a dollar for every time Spouse told her he'd be with her in a minute, "I'm just sending this e-mail." Fifteen minutes later, she'd still be waiting for him. Why couldn't the man either a) find the "send" key and hit it, or b) just be honest in the first place and tell her he is writing an e-mail and would probably need another fifteen minutes? Felicity, for whom, since becoming sober, lying is equivalent to an act of cowardice never mind disrespect, has argued the point countless times.

"And really," she'll say, "if you must lie, save it for something big, something that might save the life of another, if not your own skin."

So she's surprised to hear Spouse agree to call said collector right away. Although maybe the fact that they have teeth-cleaning appointments this morning plays a part in his forgoing the opportunity to write a novel and call it an e-mail.

She sits on the couch watching a goldfinch fly to and from its nest in the wisteria. She hears Spouse tell the collector they'd love to accept the invitation. "I wonder," he goes on, "if we could invite a friend who will be staying with us. She's really beautiful."

Felicity may have actually uttered "What the fuck!" out loud. "Are you kidding me?" She looks at the kitchen clock. They're already running late. One of the most important things Felicity learned in therapy is that timing is everything. Now that her hormones and chemistry are back in balance she is once again able to put that knowledge into practice. She knows that the conversation she needs to have with Spouse with regard to his just uttered sexist comment, will require time and patience, will more than likely involve some amount of denial and defensiveness on his part and most definitely will entail some accusation and the expression of disgust on her part. Therefore, she decides that embarking on that particular journey while hurtling along winding roads in a small metal enclosure on wheels is not the optimal time and place, especially when the destination involves having one's teeth and gums scraped to buggery by a non-English speaking hygienist wielding sharp instruments. With herculean effort, Felicity smiles at Spouse as he comes down the stairs in his jolly rooster mood asking, "Ready to go?"

If you only knew, Felicity thinks. "Yep," she says and for the next twenty minutes keeps her mouth clamped shut so tightly she thinks the dentist might have to use the jaws-of-life to pry her open.

"You're very quiet," Spouse remarks as they're driving home. "I haven't even caught a glimpse of your pearly whites."

"I'll show you mine if you show me yours," Felicity says baring hers in a smile akin to that of a possum feigning death.

"Nice," Spouse says, baring his own newly cleaned fangs in a rat-faced grin.

"All the better to eat you with," Felicity says, congratulating herself on not licking her chops.

"Everything OK?" Spouse asks, swerving to avoid an oncoming car that has taken a wicked bend a bit too wide.

"Yes," Felicity lies, feeling the lie to be justified in that it might possibly be saving both their lives while Spouse navigates that last stretch of winding road. It would be such a drag to crash so close to home and before Felicity has had the chance to metaphorically slay the rooster. "Just thinking about the novel," she adds, embroidering the truth quite nicely she thinks.

"Yeah, how's that coming along? You haven't read me anything for a while."

"It's pretty interesting," she says. "It's coming to an interesting place. Unexpected really. Maybe I'll read to you later." *After I've read you the riot act*, she thinks.

After lunch Spouse goes into the library for a Skype interview while Felicity goes upstairs to type up the latest pages she's written. As sometimes happens she's surprised at the turn the novel has taken. It feels right, timely, even though she knows she's barely scratching the surface. She isn't sure if this is because she needs to write the skeleton of what is obviously the first draft of the novel, or because she's trying to escape what she knows will be some hard shit to face and some uncomfortable truths to bare.

As she continues typing, she feels both excited and uneasy. Is she turning this into a polemic? Is she up to the demands this particular subject embodies? She'd like to think she is courageous enough to write the feminist in-your-face rant. At the same time, she hopes she is capable of nuance, of letting go of the black-and-white extremism that spews from any minority group when they've finally had enough. She also feels it will require even more courage to take a hard look at women's part in maintaining their silence for so many hundreds and thousands of years. There are, she feels, many questions to be asked on the way to truth and healing.

But for now, she is interested in hearing Spouse's response to the last few chapters. Although she has decided she won't read him the last chapter. She feels that to do so would in some way let him off the hook, would distance him from his own culpability in the patriarchy. No, she'll stop at the end of chapter 41. Perhaps unfairly lulling him into the comfort of being loved by her, even as he slept. Even on a moonless night.

43

FELICITY HAS JUST FINISHED TYPING the last sentence when Spouse emerges from the library.

"How'd the interview go?" she asks.

"Really good. She was young but she asked some really interesting questions."

Felicity wonders if the "she" had been a "he" whether Spouse would have been surprised by the combination of youth and intelligence, but decides to table that question and go directly, if not for the jugular, at least to the heart of the matter.

"Let's have a cup of tea," she suggests, putting up the kettle. "There's something I'd like to talk about."

The day has been iffy weatherwise, an unusually cool, cloudy morning had given way to a bright patch allowing them to lunch outside, but now the sky is darkening and a nearby rumble of thunder heralds rain. Just as Felicity pours the water into the teapot, the first big drops begin to splat on the patio.

"Bummer," she says. "I was so looking forward to sitting out back."

"Never mind," Spouse says. "You want to sit at the table or on the couch?"

Felicity opts for the table deciding the couch to be too comfortable.

"So, what's on your mind?" Spouse asks, as Felicity pours the tea.

"Do you remember your phone conversation this morning, about the dinner party in Paris?"

"Of course. You told me to accept the invitation, right?" His voice has the slight edge that indicates he's already afraid he's done the wrong thing.

"Right," she says. "But are you aware of how you justified Penny's right to be invited, too?"

"What *are* you talking about?" The edge is being honed now.

"Look," Felicity continues, "I'm not looking for an argument here, so please try to hear what I'm saying without jumping into defense mode, OK?"

"I knew something was up," he says. "All morning you were acting weird."

"Actually, I was not acting 'weird' and this is not about me, so please, don't go there before we've even started. My 'weird' behavior was me trying to act like an adult and not pick a fight when we were on our way to the bloody dentist."

"Oh, so this is a fight then?"

"Oh for god's sake, stop twisting this around. What I want to talk about is bigger than both of us. You asked whatever-his-name-is if we could invite Penny, right?"

"Right. And his name is Dominique."

"Okay, but before Dominique could reply, you said, and I quote, 'She's really beautiful.'"

"What's wrong with that?"

"Oh boy." Felicity shakes her head and refills their cups. "I'm not sure what's worse; that you said what you said or the fact that you have no fucking idea what the implication is."

Spouse starts to interrupt but Felicity holds up her hand. "Wait, wait. Let me ask you this. If it had been a male friend we'd wanted to invite would you have felt the need to justify his presence by saying, 'He's really handsome'?"

Spouse puts a dollop of honey in his tea and Felicity prepares to be sweet-talked. To hell with that. "Look," she says, "my point is that every man, your lovely self included, has been inducted into the patriarchy since boyhood. In your case, into the subconscious belief that women are not only second-class but their right to sit at the table depends on their looks. It's not the fact that you felt you had to justify her being invited. I get that. It's the justification you chose. I think if it had been one of our male friends we'd wanted to invite you would have said something like, 'We have a friend staying with us, could we invite him? I think you'd find him interesting.'"

"What's the difference?" Spouse asks. "Beautiful, interesting, what's the big deal?"

"Are you serious? Come on, babe, you're smarter than that. You said she was beautiful because you know every man wants a beautiful woman at his party. An interesting one, not so much. A handsome man, not so much. And let me ask you this: what if Penny wasn't physically beautiful? What if she was, according to the male eye, grossly overweight, or plain, nondescript, whatever? How would you have felt about inviting *that* woman to Mr. Wealthy Important Collector's dinner party? Would you have even wanted to invite her?"

"Of course I would," Spouse says, but Felicity knows he knows that actually he isn't sure.

"I'm really not trying to pick on you," she says.

"Well, it sure feels like you are."

"Well, it's an uncomfortable subject, isn't it? For all of us. But if you and I can't talk about this like the supposedly liberal, intelligent adults we profess to be then what the fuck? I'm trying to make a point here. I'm trying to say, look, if a basically good man like you can say such a sexist thing without even realizing it, then it just goes to show how bloody ingrained this shit is. You and other good men like you think all this #MeToo stuff has nothing to do with you and I'm telling you you're wrong. I'm telling you that what seems like a minor offense, compared to raping a woman, is actually part of the same problem. It all comes from the same belief that men are superior. That only beautiful women have the right to inclusion and that, by the way, the man will decide what beautiful is. The only difference between you and the sexual predators is that you're not mentally sick. Men's prejudicial behavior toward women has a wide range and none of it, *none* of it, is acceptable."

They sit in silence for a while. Felicity's pulse is racing; she waits for him to come up with a defense and prepares herself for round two. But the man she fell in love with three decades ago, the one who had listened to her so intently on that first evening, that man shows up now.

"You're right," he says, moving his empty cup back and forth on the table. "I hear you and I'm sorry and I don't know what to say."

Felicity looks at him, tears welling up. "Thank you. You don't have to say any more right now."

He reaches across the table and wipes the tears away. "Why are you crying?"

"Because it's such a relief to be heard." She doesn't add "finally," feeling it would be an unnecessary dig in this moment. "And because what you just said makes me love you even more. And it gives me hope."

"How do you mean?"

"Well, I think part of what makes women feel so helpless and hopeless is that when they try to have these conversations with men it's just more of the same. The man becomes defensive, the woman becomes angry, the man becomes accusatory, the woman caves. And yes, OK, I know that bit about women caving is something we women need to take a look at. I just don't think many of us really want to at the moment. We're tired. We want you all to take responsibility first, because you are the perpetrators and we are the victims."

"Do you feel like a victim?" Spouse asks, "Because I never think of you as a victim."

"Well, that's convenient for you, isn't it?"

"How so?"

"Well, once again it shows how deep this shit is. If you were willing to see the way in which I, along with every woman, am a victim then you'd have to accept that there are ways in which you've stood by and done nothing."

Spouse lets go of the cup and crosses his arms across his chest.

"Like how?"

Felicity looks at him, sees that round two has arrived and sags. She suddenly wants to make nice, to just rest in the sweet place they had just landed, as if one little mea culpa from a man should suffice. Don't push your luck; don't upset the guy. Take the little scrap and stay hungry but grateful; something's better than nothing. *But it's not*, Felicity thinks. Sometimes the "something" is a token offering; sometimes it's a form of blackmail: I'll give you this little confession and pat you on the head and now get back in your place and leave me the fuck alone or else. Yeah, she thinks, that's the way it goes. Give the little lady something and then go right back to being a superior bully. That's why women cave. The energy it takes for a woman to enter the ring and go the first round, even if she wins it, just about wipes her out. *What the fuck's with that?* she thinks. Felicity knows she'll be exploring that in the near future, but for now she's gonna man up and stay in the ring.

"Well, seeing as you asked," she says, "how about all the times you and I collaborated on a project and then when it made it out into the world I was basically erased? Either my name would be in tiny print or the publicity and press talked about how *you* made such-and-such and I never even got mentioned. Or how about when we were interviewed together for NPR then *wham!* when it aired, I was completely cut from the interview.

"Well that's not my fault," Spouse says. He's got his mouthguard in now.

"Oh, well, that's handy for you, isn't it? What about how you never stood up for me? How about after it happened, even once, you didn't make a point of telling the fuckers it was a no-go if your equal collaborator wife didn't get equal billing?"

"But I *do* do that now!" Spouse protests.

"Oh, please. You 'do it now,'" she mimics. "Why do you do it now?" she raises her hand as he starts to answer. "You do it now because I begged you to for twenty-five fucking years. That's right, shake your head. That's helpful. How do you think it felt all those years, every time you said 'I' in an interview and afterward I pretty-please reminded you that it was 'we'? Have you any idea how exhausting it is to keep sticking up for yourself, even with your own husband? To keep putting yourself back on the map you helped chart? That bullshit about how behind every great man there's a woman? Fuck that. We're all coming out of the shadows now, baby. Women are tired of doing all the mundane shit without which men would not be great. The only difference between immigrants and women like me is we can't be deported. We were relegated to the back seat centuries ago. And I have it good! Imagine how it is for immigrant women, black women, Muslim women. It only took me twenty-five years to get equal billing," she says, giving a bitter laugh. "It's bloody frightening," she says, lifting the teapot. She tips it over her cup, but it's empty.

"Do you feel frightened?" Spouse asks.

She sees the look of shock on his face. "Not like I used to be, but yes deep down I'm still frightened. You know why? Because every time a woman asks for something, she knows she runs the risk of being seen as demanding, and if she becomes too demanding, never mind the back seat, she'll be kicked out of the damn car and some new pretty young thing will be invited into the front seat . . . until *she* asks for something and then it's the back seat for her and on it goes until there are thousands of us, millions, standing by the roadside praying for a lift from someone who won't rape us. But you know what? We ain't standing by the roadside no more. We're marching."

44

THERE IS SILENCE for a while during which Felicity sits with beating heart, feeling Spouse's discomfort, revisiting the urge to take it away from him. Finally, he comes forward.

"I hear you," he says. "And that's a really powerful image."

"What is?"

"All you women, all of you, throughout history, all lined up on the road." He hesitates a moment before adding, "Coming for us."

"I'm not coming for you," she says. "Not in that way. I don't want to slay you. I want to educate you, because you're teachable. Unfortunately, the vast majority of you are not willing to be taught anything by women. That's why we need men like you. You're going to have to do your bit."

"Count me in."

She looks at him, wondering if he has any idea how long the road ahead is before men and women arrive at equality. Not in our lifetime, she thinks. But then, look at all the lifetimes that had already been lived for the cause with no end in sight. Progress not perfection? Sure, but. . . .

Spouse interrupts her thoughts. "I don't want to leave you right now but I really need to get a couple e-mails off before dinner," he says.

"That's OK. I need some quiet time to think about the novel and figure out where I'm going with it," she says.

They stand up from the table and there is an awkward moment where each wonders if it would be OK to hug the other; he because he doesn't want the hug misinterpreted as some form of condescension and she because she doesn't want it misconstrued as absolution. As it is they simultaneously reach a hand out to stroke the arm of the other before going their separate ways, Spouse to his desk and Felicity to the garden.

As she wanders the paths of the property, she thinks of all the men she's "worked" with over the past four years. Nursery men and stonemasons whose discomfort at having to take orders from a woman she's had to navigate. All of them surprised that it was she and not the man of the house who was in charge. Mostly, she's succeeded in that, and in spite of sexism and the language barrier, she's managed to make them feel comfortable with her and she's congratulated herself on this. But now, as she looks back, it pisses her off to realize that part of her success has been achieved by using her feminine wiles. First, shake their hand like a man. Then apologize for her poor language. Serve them coffee and chocolate. Praise them for the simplest accomplishment and, often, defer to their suggestions, even when it meant positioning something major like an olive tree, because she had felt it would be asking one thing too many to turn it a little to the left. And suddenly there she'd been, volunteering to sit in the back seat in order for the fucking rooster to save face. She walks to one of the olives trees behind the house and sits on the stone bench underneath.

The bench, she thinks, is a perfect example of the battle between the sexes. She'd made a clear drawing of the bench she had wanted; simple, rustic, the seat slightly curved to embrace the trunk of the tree. They'd taken the drawing to the local stoneyard. The owner, fancying himself a sculptor, nodded at the drawing. "No problem," he had declared. Four weeks later, his delivery men unloaded his interpretation of her drawing, something ridiculously ornate, a pompous perch that belonged on the grounds of a villa, not in the garden of a barn! Unable to control herself, Felicity had yelled, "Are you fucking kidding me?" her message clearly understood by the non-English speaking men who immediately became defensive even though they hadn't made the bloody thing. Who was this woman, a foreigner no less, who had the nerve to complain? Felicity, seeing where that was headed, marched into the house where she briefed Spouse and begged him to take over. Ever reasonable, he ambled out, told the men it wasn't what they had ordered, let them know it wasn't their fault and asked them to take it back, which they did.

Felicity finally got the bench she wanted because they decided it should be Spouse who dealt with the owner, who eventually personally delivered it, having by then discovered that Spouse was a famous artist. And didn't the bastard claim the design, her design, as his own creation?

Tempted to kick it, Felicity gets up from the bench and wanders over to the divan swing; another of her ideas of which she has had to remind Spouse, after overhearing him tell some visitors that "We decided this was the perfect place to put one of these." Fucking hell, but the road was long and how many women's ideas had been used by men to pave it?

But come on, Felicity, life is more nuanced than that, no? She sits on the divan and swings gently under the trees. A memory comes to her. It was the first spring they moved here. She had planted three ancient olive trees, one for each of their children, and once they were in the ground, it became obvious to her that a flight of stone steps belonged in the land sloping between two of them; four wide stone steps that would lead from the front gate down to the patio in front of the house.

On the morning that the stonemasons arrived, she made them coffee and then, wanting them to implicitly know that she was one of them, that she hadn't always lived this privileged life, she'd got down on her hands and knees and with a ridiculously small pick axe had gone to work on busting up the ground in front of the patio. This was to be the first of many flower beds and borders. The ground, more stubborn than her, was composed of gravel on top of bedrock. It took her an hour to make a hole big enough for one small plant. But, by god, she did it, flying sparks and all. By the time she finished, the men had prepared the slope for laying the stone steps. Then it was lunchtime and they drove off.

When they returned, one of them unloaded a pneumatic drill from the back of the pick up, walked to the patch in front of the patio and within fifteen minutes had turned over the ground. Together she and he removed the broken up stones and poured in the sacks of earth she had bought. Then, leaving her to her planting, he'd gone back to work with his partner.

As Felicity replays this memory she feels a bit weepy. This, then, is possible. This, too, exists: the capability for men and women to work together in kindness and respect. She gets up and goes inside, walks up the stairs and over to Spouse's desk. "A hug should never be squandered on the road to equality," she says and opens her arms as he stands up.

45

LATER THEY DO what they've been doing so well since the first week they met; they prepare dinner together while Keith Jarrett serenades them with *The Melody at Night, with You*, a title which seems fitting after an, at times, disharmonious day. The evening is a little chilly, but the air still and the garden has an hour of golden light left before sunset so they decide to eat outside. As they set the various dishes on the table, Felicity feels the diverse array could serve as a portrait of their marriage: a tapas-like spread of zucchini pasta with homemade pesto, cucumbers bathed in yogurt and mint, beets drizzled with aged balsamic and chives, and a chopped arugula salad simply dressed in olive oil and lemon, all the ingredients grown within fifty yards of where they sit. The colors, variety, and collaborative improvisation of the meal represent the best of who they are as a couple.

"Ooh, we need a touch of something dark," Felicity said, just as they are about to start. "Just to keep it real," she adds with a wicked smile. She goes back to the kitchen and returns with a small bowl of black olives. She had cured them herself last autumn, first drying them in wicker baskets in front of the fire before dividing them into two large ceramic crocks, brining them in coarse salt, turning them over every evening for two weeks until the salt became liquid. After she had drained, rinsed, and patted them dry, she put them back in the crocks and stirred them in oil, garlic, pepperoncino, and orange zest, finally spooning them into a dozen decorative jars some of which had been given as Christmas presents.

It had been a hard three years for the country's olive groves. The first year, flies had pierced every olive, depositing eggs inside, the entire harvest ruined. The second year, just as the trees came into flower, a freak hailstorm had knocked the blossoms to the ground. No blossoms, no olives. And last year, the third, many of the trees had suffered due to an unusually early, hot spring, which had seduced the flowers into making an early appearance, only to be killed off by a late frost.

Perhaps because it is in a more protected location, the tree named after Felicity's daughter has remained unharmed and is the only one in their garden, and one of the few in the whole valley, to bear olives this year. If the meal spread before Spouse and Felicity is a portrait of them, then for sure that tree is a portrait of Felicity's daughter at that time. And so she renames her child Olivia.

Before her birth, Felicity had named her Nicholas, having been sure she was carrying a boy. This certainty, obviously proven wrong at the birth, had been Felicity's first experience of maternal guilt. How could she not have known what grew within her? Had her certainty of the gender actually been a defense, a bit of magical thinking with which she unconsciously decided it was a boy, because the first, a girl, was stillborn? If she changed the sex did it have a better chance of survival, because it was easier to survive as a male than a female? Or had the strength of this fetus in utero been such a contrast to that of the first, that it was only natural to interpret that strength as masculine? Because, let's face it, women have bought into the myth of patriarchy. Whatever. Olivia, conceived on Independence Day, arrived fully fledged on the first day of spring.

From where they sit, Felicity and Spouse can see all three olive trees. In February, they had been severely pruned, Felicity having followed the advice of the farmer whose native wisdom far exceeded her own limited knowledge about these ancient beings. The farmer had been right. Now, five months later, all three are lush with new growth, and Olivia, once the weakest of them, already bears more young fruit than the others. "You go, girl," Felicity whispers.

"What?" Spouse asks.

"What are you deaf?" Felicity jokes. After five years of pretending otherwise, he'd finally relented and been fitted with a pair of hi-tech hearing aids just a few weeks ago. Five years she'd begged him to do this. Five years of having to say everything twice and being blamed for not speaking clearly, which, in itself, was ripe coming from an American, and her speaking the Queen's English. But never mind. She is done with resentment.

"I was just thinking of Olivia," she continues. "And how much her tree has paralleled her life these last few years."

"That's interesting. How do you mean?"

"Well, remember how healthy it was when it first arrived here? Then when Olivia started getting really sick, the tree started dropping its leaves and nothing I planted under it survived. Yet in spite of all its suffering it bore fruit."

Suddenly she bursts into tears. "Fuck. Fuck-fuck-fuck."

"What is it?" Spouse asks scooting along the bench to put his arm around her. "What's wrong?"

"I just realized why I've been so stuck with the novel this week," she said, blowing her nose on the napkin. "I thought it was because all this 'me too' stuff was going nowhere, but it's her. Olivia. She wants in. I was determined not to bring her into this. I thought I was protecting her, but really I was just avoiding the whole thing. But now, now that she's getting strong again, she doesn't want to be protected. And anyway, it's bullshit. It's me I'm trying to protect."

"From what?"

"The truth," she says.

46

TWO YEARS EARLIER Olivia had nearly died. Coinfections from a disease that had been misdiagnosed more than a decade earlier had invaded nearly every system in her body, gradually bringing her to the brink. Hospitalized for three days and insisting that there was no need for her mother to rush to her side, Felicity had shamefully chosen to believe her daughter rather than follow her own instincts and so had not arrived in New York until three days later. By that time her daughter was back in her apartment, further allowing Felicity to indulge in denial as to the seriousness of the situation.

Nothing could have prepared her for the shock of seeing the woman who opened the door. Her beautiful, bold, robust Olivia stood there like a frail bird, bones and fear protruding from her.

Over the course of the following two months, as Felicity helped her daughter back to life, they learned how to be the mother and daughter they'd each wanted. There was, after all, nothing like a near-death experience for stripping away fiction.

It's been a week since Felicity and Spouse were dining outside, days that Felicity has spent coming up to the edge of her secret and then frighteningly, consciously, backing away. She has distracted herself with the Wimbledon finals and a three-day visit with friends, during which time she has not only chatted and laughed but has so far removed herself from that which she does not want to admit. So disconnected she has been that for the first time in forty-seven years, the birthday of her stillborn child has passed without commemoration. The guilt Felicity feels about this is so crippling that she further distracts herself by digging out half the plants from the flower bed in front of the patio.

For weeks she has looked at this bed seeing, knowing, that it is out of control. Has felt almost panicked looking at nepita, lavender, and lemon verbena that have sprawled beyond their beauty, reaching out to suffocate one another, some of them lying down in flat surrender. And each time she's looked at the bed, she's been unable to find her way in. What should be removed? What should be saved? And if she tended to it now would it be a kindness or an unsurvivable trauma in the heat of summer? Finally she'd gone to work, starting with the plants beyond help, yanking them ruthlessly, leaving only those whose merit was obvious: cascading rosemary, chives, thyme, and the central bush whose name she has been unable to discover and so has called it a flowering black currant as it resembles a so-named plant her mother had grown in the front garden of her childhood. Once the weak and diseased plants were removed, Felicity had felt sorrow for the now-diminished bed. How could it have gone from being a showstopper last year to a tangle of weak stems this year? This morning she had dug in some more thyme, oregano, and parsley, deciding to fill the spaces with life-affirming plants.

Now, fully aware of the metaphoric meaning of that labor, she sits under the oak tree hoping to find the courage to write about the act she still finds unforgivable. As she starts to write of her child nearly dying, she feels overwhelmed. *Bloody hell*, she thinks, embarking on this feels like it could be a novel unto itself.

It's July, nearly August. It's hot and humid and a restless wind is on the prowl. For fuck's sake, Felicity, what a coward you are. Do you think that writing about how close you and your daughter became during those months that you helped nurse her back to the living, do you think writing about that will let you off the hook? That you will be absolved of the dreadful decision you made all those years ago? Dream on. You don't get to speak of redemption yet. Here's the thing, Felicity, and you can forget about the bad behavior of others. Your business is this: What responsibility do you bear for losing custody of your child?

The wind is becoming ferocious, gusts of it swirling around Felicity where she sits on the divan swing. Bits of dried debris from the tree fall on her. Ants are already forming a line along the edge of the cushion. The hydrangeas are drooping in their pots and Felicity almost gets up to water them. Stay the fuck where you are, Felicity.

Time to tell the truth.

She uncaps her pen.

"I asked her father to come and get her," she writes. "I asked him to come and get her two weeks before she was due to return to him for a visit. I did this because . . .

Because I lost my job.

Because on the same day my landlord raised my rent.

Because I couldn't cope.

Because I was lonely.

Because I had no one to turn to.

Because . . ."

Because, Felicity, you had just picked up your three-year-old from nursery school. You were driving home with her. . . .

Her pen runs out of ink at the same time that she runs out of pages. She inserts a new cartridge and opens a new blank book.

This would be the perfect moment to wipe the slate clean, she thinks, just, you know, admit it to yourself and move on. But Felicity has been writing for fifty years and so she knows the power of putting things in writing.

Felicity lost custody of her child because when she was driving up the hill to their little apartment she saw the most amazing creature walking ahead of her.

More than six feet of magical masculinity clad in black. A dancer's body full of grace and mystery. A bright piece of fabric is wound around his head. A bag of tribal cloth slung easily over his shoulder reveals the tops of three bamboo flutes. She rolls down the window and hears the tinkling chatter of a tambourine. "Can I give you a lift?" she calls. He turns his noble face to her, his skin almost as black as his clothes, and the spell is cast.

She takes him home and while she makes dinner he takes one of his handmade flutes and makes music for Olivia, who, interestingly, is not seduced by him. After she puts Olivia to be bed he tells that he's leaving for Mexico next week, why doesn't Felicity join him? Why not indeed? She will be unemployed next week and she can't afford the new rent. She'd only have Olivia for another two weeks anyway so, what would be so wrong about returning the child to her father a week or so early?

This is what's wrong with that, Felicity: You chose to be with a stranger instead of your child.

Say it again, you pathetic woman.

I chose to be with a man instead of with my child.

Say it again.

Say it ten times.

Say it.

Say it.

I chose a man over my child; I chose a man over my child; I chose a man over my child.

The wind has stopped.

The cicadas are rubbing their wings together in a ceaseless chide.

Her mouth is dry.

The cicadas stop.

The birds stop.

The line of ants continues.

Shame rises taking her breath with it.

She will not cry.

She does not deserve the rescue.

She sits with her guilt and, as the wind returns, she writes again:

"I chose to run away with a man instead of staying with my daughter."

The why, the how are out of reach and must stay that way for now. If she could, she would bind herself to the divan swing and repeat her sin until she has embodied the truth of it. Oh, wretched, wretched soul, be still and know the dark stone in your heart.

Felicity had sat there for how long? An hour? Time, always impossible to measure, now wrapped itself around her like a warped screen. A flashback arose. A psilocybin trip back in the seventies when, just as she thought she'd finally lost her mind, convinced she was about to become a permanent resident of Hollywood Hospital, she had instead watched the contents of a packet of sugar cascade in slow motion, as if from a great height; the granules leaving her hand and falling, falling into the milky coffee where she watched the chemistry of every single grain take what appeared to be minutes to dissolve; the independence of each grain losing itself as it integrated with the liquid. She had watched in wonder as the dissolution of time revealed how little we see, how utterly ignorant we are of the minutiae of life, the tick-tock of time hurrying us forward, robbing us of untold marvels and deeper truths.

Now, released from its packet, her secret was revealed to her. What had, over the intervening forty-two years, reared up now and again like an unwanted flashback, a visual image of a stranger clad in black, was now a confession. Until now, each time she'd seen him walking up that hill, panic had arisen, followed by instant suppression, so that until this day she had never formed all the granules into a sentence. *The* sentence.

"I chose a man over my child."

Every letter of every word a grain of truth falling slowly into place.

She does not search for excuses. Nor does she seek comfort or relief. She doesn't want to dwell on it, but *in* it. No words of recrimination or judgment arise. She has lived the flagellation all this time. This awful secret. Where has it paced within her? She has an image of it shattered, the words broken into shards, into tiny pieces and finally into dust; her own nuclear fallout swept into every organ, every cell. Small puffs of it exhaled with every subsequent truth she's told in her oh-so-sober effort to become an honest person.

Another gust of wind shivers the oak leaves. A blue-black cloud spreads like a bruise over the hills and suddenly she's sitting at a table on a screened porch. It's 1989. She's seven months sober. She's doing it all by the book, literally. A meeting every day, sometimes two. Three on really bad days when she has no fucking idea whatsoever who she is or what she's doing. Clinging to the Steps, the axioms, the stories. Those early weeks and months, veering between terror and relief. Sudden glimpses of what might be possible living life sober, just as quickly snatched away by a jealous disease telling her she'd never make it. And she knows they're right, all those fellow alcoholics who tell her that the bastard disease is out there in the parking lot doing push-ups, waiting. That terrifies her more than the thought of never having another drink. Ever. For as long as she lives.

So she does it by the book. Open meetings, closed meetings, Big Book meetings, Twelve-Step meetings. She gets a sponsor the first week who takes her over to a table laden with pamphlets and books. "Read these," she'd said, loading her up with AA literature. Literature? She looks at it all and asks her first sober question. "Can I read novels, too?"

Under the sponsor's guidance, Felicity embarks on the Steps. Step Four: *Make a searching and fearless inventory of ourselves.* Step Five: *Admit to God, to ourselves, and to another human being the exact nature of our wrongs.*

Here she is, mid-summer, exactly twenty-nine years ago, sitting on her sponsor's porch admitting her sins. She tells her of the money she stole from her mother in order to buy sweeties. Of the money she stole from her London flatmate's handbag in order to buy cigarettes. Of the money she stole from Spouse Number Four to buy coke. The coke dealer she jerked off for a few "free lines." The people she's judged and ridiculed. The husband she tried to steal from his sweet, loving wife. The people she befriended for momentary gain. The countless lies, to parents, bosses, friends, lovers. The men she's fucked in the name of love and, yes, the abortions. She tells it all, a lifetime of desperate wrongs piling up on the table between her and the sponsor, the sweet afternoon turning sulphurous, thunder rolling, rain driven by a savage wind, and the sponsor sitting quietly, like the angel of redemption.

Felicity remembers the feeling of relief, the amount of it small in comparison to the enormity of her sins. Well, of course, Felicity, of course, because your inventory actually wasn't *completely* searching and fearless was it? You shared only that which you could bear. You left the biggie off the list. Now here it stands, alone, front and center, the words fully formed, out in the open. Oh, but they're not are they, Felicity? They're not all out in the open. So you finally admitted it to yourself. Well-done. No small thing. But what now?

With a shock Felicity realizes she's going to have to tell Spouse. She begins a conversation with herself; she tries on a couple of possibilities like, I don't have to tell him, or at least not now. But neither bear weight and as if she's called his name he appears, coming round the corner of the house with a sunny smile on his face. Then he sees the pen in her hand. "Oh, sorry," he says and turns to leave.

"No," she calls. "Don't go."

47

THEY SIT TOGETHER on the swing as they have so many times, at opposite ends, backs to the cushioned arms, legs stretched out toward each other. Later, she will wonder why she read her confession to him, instead of just telling it. When she finishes there is silence. It takes her close to a minute before she can raise her head and look him in the eye. He waits until she does and then he nods.

"That took a lot of courage," he says. She searches his face . . . for what? Some hint of judgment, disappointment, perhaps a lessening of his esteem for her? But what she sees is matter of fact: He loves her nonetheless. As if to prove that history repeats itself, thunder begins a slow rumble but instead of rain there is a faint tinkle of sheep bells as a flock makes its way across the fields, down to the road where it will soon flow like a river of wool in search of greener pasture. The sky darkens and Felicity longs for the sheep to enlighten this passage, a beam of innocence in her own dark history.

Spouse starts to say something but she hushes him.

"Don't forgive me," she says.

"What's to forgive?" he says. "I see only the pain and desperation and the confusion of what your life was back then."

"You are the dearest, kindest man," she says. "But I have to stay in the bare light of this for a while. I know that eventually I must have mercy and compassion for myself, but not yet."

"Do you feel relieved?" he asks.

"Not yet. I just feel the enormity of it. The enormity of the responsibility I bear for that decision and the enormity of the space it's taken up in me all these years. It's strange," she says. "It's as though it's both in me and out of me at the same time. I housed it for forty-two years. I housed a secret the way a murderer buries the body in the basement. You could say I've unearthed the truth and it ain't pretty."

The sheep bells have ceased, as has the wind. And then, suddenly, the sky cracks open above them. They rush to cover the swing with a tarpaulin, fighting against great gusts of wind. Spouse runs to the car to roll up the windows while Felicity grabs the laundry off the line just as the first drops of rain begin. They run to the house and get inside just as the wind roars down from the north, sheets of rain mixed with hail bend every living thing toward the earth. The house is in darkness even though it's only late afternoon. They turn on lights only to have them extinguished as a flash of lightning cuts the power.

"Wow," Spouse says, "that wasn't in the forecast."

"You can say that again," Felicity says.

Over the next few days, Felicity will veer from feeling light and energized to feeling heavy and deeply tired, as if she is both the calm and the storm. She will belatedly light a candle for her first-born and wonder when she will share the truth with the daughter who once was lost to her and with whom she now shares a profound bond. She will wait, for both their sakes, until the bond carries more history. For if a secret eats at the soul, so the truth can unravel a tapestry before it is freed from the loom.

48

IT'S BEEN A WEEK since Felicity revealed her secret and she is still in limbo. As she sits at her desk wondering where to go from here, she distracts herself by contemplating the word "limbo." Such a deceptive word, "limbo." It sounds so relaxing, almost carefree, a ridiculous dance craze even, in which one bends over backward in order to shimmy under a horizontal bar. Huh! She's bending over backward all right, in order to shimmy under the guillotine of her own judgment. She writes down "limbo"and further distracts herself by inventing mnemonics. The first one that comes to mind is:

Like
It's
My
Bloody
Onus

Followed by:

Laughter
Is
My
Bogus
Operandi

She's getting into it now:

Life
Is
Mostly
Bad
Odor

Although she prefers:

Lust
Is
Mostly
Bought
Online

Or, hopefully:

Look
It
Might
Be
OK

But it isn't. It isn't OK. She is living in the literal definition of limbo, existing between heaven and hell. Zombieland. Every day, when she awakes, there is a moment of confusion, as if there is something important to remember. It had been like that when her baby died. Months of awakening to a feeling of urgency. Knowing there was something different about the day; a split second of hopeful anticipation followed by the horrific knowledge that what was different was that her baby was dead. Again. Now, when she wakes up, there is a momentary pause before she descends once more into limbo. She feels deadened, flattened by the truth. She can't even cry, although she longs to. Maybe two or three times every day she feels the tears start and then her body reabsorbs them before they have a chance to spill.

On her desk is a quote from Isak Dinesen: "The cure for anything is saltwater: sweat, tears, or the sea."

Foolproof cures which Felicity has employed for years. But now? What, no tears, Felicity? But you have a Ph.D. in crying, what gives? Nothing. Nothing gives. She's not even treading water. She is a stagnant pond. And she can't figure it out. Is she unable to cry because she feels undeserving of release? Or, perhaps, because if she starts, she will never stop? Or because this time it will not be a cure? She is stunned by the truth, and if she thought that the hiding of it for decades had been a prison of her own making, now she is in purgatory. It's as though something painful has been extracted but the gaping hole has been immediately filled in. By what? Shame? Horror? Shock? Yes, maybe that; the shock of discovering not only the act of abandonment she committed but that it's who she was then. As though that single act defines her. And there's this: Back then, when she had fairly recently found out that her blood mother had abandoned her, Felicity had, in her own way, done exactly the same thing to her own daughter . . . and hadn't even known that was what she was doing! How could that be? How can she find solace? Must she forever remain guilty? Can she allow herself to see that she had been so damaged by loss that she had to find, unconsciously, ways of losing all that she loved before it was taken from her? Can she bear to feel the sorrow that links her mother to her and her to her own daughters? Cry, goddamn it, cry. Get it over and done with.

But she knows it can never be over and done with. The past is irretrievable, irreparable, but never irrelevant. At what point does a person let go of having suffered injustices and cruelties and just snap the fuck out of it and go forward? Maybe that's it, Felicity thinks. Maybe the tears belong to the past. Maybe the way out of limbo is to say:

Love
Is
My
Best
Offer

50

FELICITY SPENDS A COUPLE OF DAYS reading over the sixty-five thousand words she has written in the last year and a half and judges them to be both entirely too much and not nearly enough. Where is the arc? Where are the people for god's sake? There used to be so many people and now . . . ? It's as though there are two halves to her adult life; the half before she broke her neck and the half after.

Before she broke her neck there were many, many people. The lovers, the drunks, the addicts, more lovers, and gradually friends, the ones you can count on. And then had come the clients. All those heads of hair walking into her salon five days a week for seven years. Every one of them a story. In fact, they had peopled her first novel. They were the loved and the lonely, the shy and the demanding. They were the curly, straight, permed, highlighted, bobbed and layered, braided, shagged, pixied, buzzed and asymmetrical, thick and thin. They were raven, chestnut, auburn, flame, titian, mousey, blonde, gray, white, and platinum.

And under each head of hair lay the stories. The woman whose husband was whittling his way to death by cancer as she ate her way to her oblivion. There was the woman whose life had seemed so perfect until she came to Felicity one day and, after years of requesting just a trim of her New England pageboy, sat shampooed and draped in the chair, and without looking at Felicity asked her to make her look young and sexy, before bursting into tears.

This was back in the day when you could still get off an airplane before it left the gate. Which is exactly what this woman's husband had done the week before Christmas. Buckled in and ready for the Bahamas, he'd suddenly turned to her and said, after thirty married years and two grown kids, "I can't do this anymore." And with that he unbuckled himself and left her there on the runway while he went off to his new life and new wife-to-be.

There was the shy adolescent boy whose bowl cut she'd carefully trimmed every six weeks for two years, making sure to leave the bangs almost covering his eyes. Then, on his sixteenth birthday, he'd looked her straight in the eye and said, "Mohawk me."

There was the meek woman who came to Felicity one Valentine's Day, shedding hair and tears when Felicity asked if she had something special planned for the evening. "I've never had a Valentine," she whispered as the tears slipped from downcast eyes. Felicity had given her the haircut for free and a hug to go with it. And that was the last she saw of her until five years later when, flat on her back in hospital with a newly broken neck, the woman had appeared with a posy of autumn roses from her garden. "I've never forgotten what you did for me," she said.

There was the actor and the playwright and the photographer; men who came for her skill and the nearness of her. The timid young bride marched in by her macho fiancé who instructed Felicity as to what he wanted for his bride, his need almost a threat and yet, forty-five minutes later when he roared into the parking lot in his souped-up pick-up, he strode into the salon and saw her standing there shyly waiting for him. He had stood paralyzed for a moment before gently holding her face in his hands. "You are so beautiful to me," he'd whispered.

During those years, before she sobered up, Felicity was the big fish in a little pond, recognized everywhere she went. She was the wild one who could tame any head of hair. She was the fun one who, after a few drinks and a couple of lines, would sit at any piano in any bar or restaurant and play from the crevices in her heart. She was the one who outdanced everyone. The sexy clown who could have a whole bar in stitches and then go home and paint a canvas that she would sell from her salon. Before that, she was the one who outgrew the parking lot bums and Thursday night Woodstock poetry readings. She was the one who married Spouse Number Three because he'd sat next to her on the piano stool at the local bar and sang along to her music. So, duh, obviously they were meant for each other. She called it her best wedding and worst marriage. Ending it six weeks later, when she went home to change her apron for the next shift in the next restaurant and found him on their bed in her knickers and shoes jerking off. Which, actually, had made his having spat in her face during intercourse on their honeymoon night suddenly seem quaint. She is the one who survived having the shit beaten out of her by a paranoid lover, hiding out in a cabin in the woods under threat of death. Waiting for the case to go to court. Waiting for her face to heal. She is the one who drank her way up to the higher echelons of Hudson Valley society, marrying passionately, recklessly, Spouse Number Four. Her life becoming peopled with success and dinner parties and so what if her stepson hated her and her ten-year-old daughter sleepwalked in terror? Everything passes. And it did. Another marriage come and gone. Not that she was guilt-free, but at least, unlike him, she never fucked his best friend.

Then she got sober and her life became peopled with recovering alcoholics and addicts in church basements and back rooms of libraries. Her story became part of the lineage of drunk-a-logues. Days counted, then weeks and months. Finally, a whole year. And for the first time in her life she belonged, accepting applause for another sober day and giving it to the newcomers, her heart breaking along with everyone else's in the room when word came that someone had gone back out after a month or two, or a year, or twenty. Scary and heartbreaking. That old disease out in the parking lot. . . .

By the time she broke her neck, she had twenty months sober and a man who would become Spouse Number Five. She also had fifteen people a day telling her how fabulous she was; she who held their heads like babies at the font, shampooing the scalps of the tense, the fearful, the defended, the desperate, the unloved, the unfulfilled. Draping and sectioning them. Feeling the weight of their hair, the bend of it, the thick and the thin of it. The cowlicks, the wayward curls, the sparse patch carefully tended. The encouragement to try something new, to trust her, to let her reveal each person to the fullest of their supreme being, accentuate the cheek bones, reveal the shell pink ears, distract from the weak chin, apply a dash of color to the waiting lips. Tell the husband, boyfriend, boss to fuck himself. And she'd whisk off the cape like a magician, revealing the new them and in that moment they were more than they ever thought they could be and she loved every one of them.

And then it was over. Broken neck. Damaged arms. Fused C4 through C7. No more haircutting. No more big canvases. Everything gone; car, work, clients, all gone. But her man stayed. And a few friends.

There were a few weeks after the accident when all her clients and her fellows from the rooms rallied round. Many of them cooking, visiting, cleaning, shopping, driving her to the doctor. But everything passes.

Her child graduated high school and left for Europe. The clients, finally accepting she would never be giving them another haircut, gradually drifted away. So she sold her house and moved to the edge of the sea and waited to find out who next she would be.

A writer, it seems. Living life alone at a desk, peopling her new world with fictitious characters whom she grooms and tends and loves. People she believes in but who have nothing to offer her. There are no compliments at the end of a day of writing. No thank yous.

Felicity would like you to know that she still has several good friends. They e-mail and Skype and FaceTime and text and every once in a while they come visit, here on this isolated farm in another country, in another language. For a few days, she revels in the taste of English as the words round themselves in her mouth flowing fluently; thoughts and ideas heard and received, exchanged, agreed or disagreed with, added on to, exclaimed at, laughed at. The occasional sharing of a tear, but not so much. Everything passes. The friends leave, the sheep *baa*, the pen scratches across the page.

51

WHEN OLIVIA NEARLY DIED. . . .

Felicity writes those words, stops, and stares at them.

When Olivia nearly died . . . what?

Felicity showed up. That's what. In a way, she thinks now, it was similar to when Olivia was newborn and every time she woke up crying Felicity had experienced dread and duty. There was never any question of whether or not to go to her baby girl, pick her up, feel the joy of her, nurse her, coo to her, and soothe her back to sleep. But the initial feeling was always one of dread; dread that she wasn't capable of doing the right thing . . . of being a mother. After all, who had taught her how? So when Olivia nearly died, there was no question that she would show up and there was also the same fear that she wouldn't be able to do the right thing. What if she couldn't save her? But there was a difference between then and now; now her daughter was an adult who could, and did, tell Felicity what she needed from her. She was also an adult who finally needed a mother. And so, in those months of fright, of visits to doctors, of tests, of putting one foot slowly in front of the other on a daily basis of shared tears and meditation, they learned how to be a mother and daughter.

Felicity despises the saying that everything happens for a reason. What utter bullshit. Things happen. Period. Full stop. What she does believe is that when things happen, all right, let's say it like it is, when shit happens, how you choose to respond to it can make or break you. The way in which Olivia has responded to living with a chronic disease is, to Felicity, awe-inspiring. Her willingness to accept reality perhaps being the most impressive. Courage, too. Enormous courage. Humor, research, meditation. Sometimes lying incapacitated on the floor for days. Needles and tests, supplements, infusions, colonics. You name it, she has it, deals with it, moves on, until the next relapse.

She handled it better than Felicity. Even though in the depths of her terror that she wouldn't survive, Olivia told her she would channel Felicity surviving her broken neck. Does everything have to be fucking broken in order to form a bond? That bond between mother and child? You can cut the cord, but not the connection. You can be at odds with each other for years, but you'll still long for it to be otherwise.

And yes, damn right, Felicity was angry. She was angry for her child and angry for herself. What's the fucking deal? Two hopeless mothers she'd had. And two daughters, one dead and the other nearly. And this is what mothers do: They try to suck the poison out of their child. Felicity knows, now, that for two years she was unconsciously internalizing her child's disease. Give it to me. Give it to me. Let her go. And she would fret daily, agonize, try to find a miracle cure. Every day a part of her mind given over to this task of making her child well. As the days and months went by, not only could she not cure her child, but she, herself, became weaker. This is why the collapse, this is why she became ill herself. She was trying to do the impossible, animal thing that mothers do: die for her child. How many times in the last two years has Felicity fallen to her knees sobbing, give it to me, give it to me?

Oh, and let's take a moment to talk about the horror, the inefficiency, the denial, the ignorance, the ego, the greed of the American medical system. The health coverage that covers nothing. The patronizing male doctors who never listen to the patient, especially if she's a woman. Because the doctor knows everything. The exorbitant cost of treatments and medications and supplements, all out of pocket, and too bad if you or your parents can't afford them. Suffer. Suffer. Suffer some more and listen to them tell you it's your own fault. Or that you're imagining it. That there's nothing wrong with you. And you go from doctor to doctor to specialist to clinic following the carrot only to find there is no there *there*.

Felicity watches in amazement as her Olivia navigates all of this becoming, in the process, her own healer. And finally, finally, after Felicity had felt herself on the verge of collapse again, overcome by helplessness, draining herself of her own health in the vain attempt to heal her child, finally, she understands what her true job is. She learns to let go of her daughter's disease. She learns that the bond is irrefutable. She learns that it is not her job to save her daughter and that to let go of that illusion is not a form of abandonment but actually a form of respect. She's learned that she had, in some ways, infantilized her adult daughter in the futile attempt to be the mother Olivia had needed as a child. She learns that she will have to live with that regret. She learns how to be an adult mother to an adult daughter and learns that in order to best show up, she needs to be whole in herself. To be separate and strong so that never again will her daughter feel like she is a burden. Oh, grace. Oh, gratitude. Oh, sadness in place of anger, and also in place of anger . . . space. Space for possibility without expectation. Space for communication uncluttered by the past. Space to heal, as best one can, in the moment. Space to listen, to hear, to wait, to not know, to validate, to congratulate. Space to laugh. Space to meditate upon the fear of death.

What Felicity learns is that the possibility of losing another child is beyond her control and that therefore to live in fear of that is a total waste of time. There is no universal scale measuring out equal amounts of pain to each of us. Shit actually does happen. More to some than to others. There is no *reason* for that. You take an extra sip of coffee, walk down the street and a piece of masonry falls on your fucking head. That coffee had better have been outrageously good.

Felicity feels herself coming to the end of something. Is it the novel? Life? Or is it the end of her search for the beginning of her rage? The truth is, she has no idea when it started. She doubts it was when her blood mother walked away. No. That would have been shock and desolation. She also knows she can't blame it all on men, although they carry a great deal of it. Her adoptive mother, herself enraged? Sure, she got the ball rolling all right, as did her father's cowardice. Did she become enraged when her mother called her a whore right after telling Felicity she was adopted, right after Felicity had lost her first child and her father? Probably not. More shock than anything and the pain of such cruelty. Did it make her angry that her parents watched her leave at sixteen, totally ill-equipped and lacking money? No, just more sadness and the feeling of having been put up with for sixteen years and now good riddance.

Felicity knows now that she is not blameless. Knows that some of her anger must be attributed to the ways in which she feels she failed her daughter and herself.

And yes, some of the rage comes from the abuse she's taken from men. The husband who witnessed her agony when their first child died and then took the second one away. The doctor who delivered her of the dead child extinguishing her from consciousness so that she would never see or hold that child. The men who fired her because she wouldn't fuck them. The lawyer who refused to help her because she was poor. The lawyer who was friends with the judge. The men who beat her. The one who raped her. Oh, never mind . . . the list is too long. The anger righteous. But it's never that simple. There are the evil women, too. There are thousands of years of women who went along with it all. Didn't question. Didn't fight. Chose to live in submission rather than die for equality. And how could so many of us have suppressed our intelligence in order to believe we were second class? If men were the bullies, were we the cowards?

Felicity hopes the current uprising of women will eventually make a difference, but she has no expectation of this, certainly not in her lifetime. It would seem that fear increases with the population. And, from observing the way in which the younger generation is attached to digital reality, she can well imagine artificial intelligence becoming the next stage of evolution. So why waste more time being angry? The sand is running ever faster through the neck of the hourglass. Somewhere her days are numbered.

Soon she will leave her desk and go into the garden. She will bend to the earth and pull some weeds. She will catch a waft of rose perfume as the last ray of sunlight heats its petals. She will pluck and prune and plan for autumn planting. She'll wander the paths, inspecting every growing thing like a nurse in the ward of the newborn. She will once in a while look up and out to the hills and see the wind animating the wheat; a cloud darkening a field; the sun illuminating the earth from within. A sudden rainstorm, a rainbow, the sweet smell of newly mown grass, the sound of a lamb calling for its mother.

She will do these things, look at these things, smell and hear these things and then she will return to the house, to her Spouse, his eyebrows arched in boyish wonder. They will make dinner. She will read to him. They will talk. One of the kids will Skype. A friend will stop by. They will find the words they need in the new language. They will laugh at the attempt. They will floss and brush their teeth and cream their aging faces. They will get into bed and read for five minutes and then they will utter their love for each other. He will turn over, but not away, and she will spoon him and for a brief moment the moon will illuminate the neck of the man she loves.

ACKNOWLEDGMENTS

I always struggle with writing acknowledgments, as though the many months, or in this case, two and a half years, that it takes to hone language, ideas, and imagination in the crafting of a novel leaves me without adequate words with which to express my gratitude and thanks to so many people. So let me be brief.

My thanks to early readers for their support and encouragement go to: Missy O'Shaunessy, Madeleine Colvin, Brenda Bufalino, Kate Kirkwood, Sharon Mrozinski, Lorenzo Braca, Phoebe Lark Heelas, Joshua Kersha Jara, Vanessa and Chris Ryan, Vivian Ubell, and David Sumberg.

I am deeply indebted to Rose Gaete of The Literary Consultancy for her deep read and assessment of an early draft. Without her belief in this novel and her insightful editorial suggestions, Felicity would not be where she is today.

To my brilliant copy editor, Barbara Richard, thank you for standing by me, for your honesty and your kindness. Thanks also to Christopher Zucker for his elegant text design and ontime delivery.

To Bert Shaw, my thanks for planting a seed so very many years ago and helping me bring it into the light.

And most of all, and always, to my dear, ever-patient husband, Joel Meyerowitz, who listened to every word, read each draft, lifted me out of despair, expressed unbiased opinions to the extent possible for a loved one, and took quite a lot on the chin from Felicity. Thank you.

Lightning Source UK Ltd.
Milton Keynes UK
UKHW011816231119
354071UK00002B/153/P